BUSTED SYNAPSES

Broken Eye Books is an independent press, here to bring you the odd, strange, and offbeat side of speculative fiction. Our stories tend to blend genres, highlighting the weird and blurring its boundaries with horror, sci-fi, and fantasy.

Support weird. Support indie.

brokeneyebooks.com
twitter.com/brokeneyebooks
facebook.com/brokeneyebooks
instagram.com/brokeneyebooks
patreon.com/brokeneyebooks

BUSTED SYNAPSES
by ERICA L. SATIFKA

Published by
Broken Eye Books
www.brokeneyebooks.com

All rights reserved.
Copyright © 2020 Broken Eye Books and the author.
Cover illustration by Carolina Rodriguez Fuenmayor
Cover design by Scott Gable
Interior design by Scott Gable
Editing by Scott Gable

978-1-940372-58-7 (trade paperback)

BUSTED SYNAPSES

erica l. satifka

SHIT," DALE SAYS, GETTING HIS KEYS OUT AGAIN. "FORGOT MY SMOKES."

Jess tugs at his sleeve. "I'll buy you some. You can call it your birthday present."

"What about the tickets?"

"I can get you more than one present, Dale."

Dale pushes her off with a smile and heads back inside. Jess pulls her light jacket tighter around her. The lights of what passes for downtown Wheeling are going out, and by the time they get to the theater, the previews will have already started.

And that's when Jess sees it. A New Woman toddling down the street, its eyes roving over its surroundings as if the town around it is something new and strange. It's dressed in a crisply ironed blazer and skirt, its dark brown hair pulled back in a bun, its skin an even copper with no blemish.

A New Person in Wheeling, West Virginia. Jess can't help but stare.

"See, told you it wouldn't take long." An unlit cigarette dangles from Dale's lip. "Who's that?"

"Let's just go."

"Hey, you!" The woman-thing turns its head. Dale lights the cigarette. "Are you lost?"

"*Now*, Dale."

"I think she's lost." Jess tries to pull Dale away again, but he's become a rock.

"Excuse me." It's in front of both of them now. "Can you tell me where River Road is?" Its voice is halting with long gaps in it.

They talk like stroke victims, Jess thinks. *Can't get that part right. Yet anyway.*

Dale wrenches his way out of Jess's grasp. "Sure, you just take a right at the end of this street and a left once you get to the mini-mart. Can't miss it."

"Thank you," the New Woman says. It rolls its eyes back in their sockets slightly and continues down the road, legs pumping like a metronome.

Jess snorts.

"See, that didn't take so long."

"Why did you help it?"

Dale stops short. "You're being a—"

"That's *not* a person."

"Isn't that a matter of opinion?"

Jess shakes her head. "Forget it. Let's just get in the truck." She doesn't even want to go to the movies anymore. *But I will,* she thinks. *I already bought the tickets.*

The truck rumbles to life beneath them. They don't talk the whole way to the theater, and when it's over, Jess doesn't even remember what the movie was about.

JESS PINCHES HERSELF AWAKE AND STARTS ANOTHER INTRICATE DOODLE IN her sketch pad. The phones of the local branch of the Solfind Remote Call Center have rung exactly three times today, and none of them came through on her line. Jess feels a yawn coming on and bites down on her pen to stifle it.

"Excuse me, where is the personnel office?"

The halting, formal-sounding voice echoes across the open-plan office, and Jess's body shoots up straight. She isn't tired anymore.

One of her coworkers, Larry or Barry or some name like that, points to a door. The woman-thing nods, smiles, and knocks.

"What is that *thing* doing here?" Jess doesn't normally talk to the woman who sits next to her, but it's out before she can stop herself.

Gretchen frowns. "Can't possibly be asking for a job."

"Who let it in here? Why?"

"Maybe this is the end." Gretchen shrugs and picks up her knitting. "Probably shutting us down." She says it calmly, like she doesn't care.

Jess turns away and taps her pen on the handbook. She tries not to look too closely at the door to Kathy the supervisor's office. *They can't be hiring a New Woman for a call center. That's a waste. Islands don't waste.* After an interminable amount of time, the door opens, and the woman-thing and Kathy exit. They shake hands.

"Not looking good," Jess says to Gretchen. But her coworker's needles keep clacking away, the orange scarf attached to them getting incrementally longer every day.

The New Woman surveys the office, its eyes eventually falling on Jess. There's a slight flash of recognition, and then the woman-thing leaves.

Jess stands up, the folding chair that passes for a seat collapsing behind her. "I'm going to the bathroom."

"But what if you get a call?"

Jess puts her graffitied handbook inside her desk. "I'm not getting a call."

She throws the lock on the door and whips out her phone. *That thing we saw on your birthday is at my office.*

The New Woman? Dale replies.

I think they gave it a job.

There is a short break. Dale must be in the middle of an order. *They don't live here. They live in Islands.*

That was how it usually went anyway. New workers to replace old; "people" that never wore out or aged or got sick or lodged complaints. A new kind of human for a new kind of world. The propaganda campaign had gone on for so long that most people in Islands, and even outside of them, believed it.

Can I come over later? she writes.

Sorry, have a game.

Jess rolls her eyes. *Thanks anyway.* Jess shuts the phone and goes back out to the floor.

It's almost four, which means it's almost time to leave, which means another night in the basement waiting for morning. Jess makes a note to pick up something for dinner. She doubts her mother left the house all day.

DALE SPRAYS CLEANER ON THE GRILL AND ATTACKS IT WITH THE SPONGE. Hamburger grease comes off in cakey sheets, and his stomach flips over. The combined stench of low-grade meat and caustic chemicals wafts over him like a poisonous cloud.

"Quitting time."

Dale snaps his head up, banging it on the neon-bright cupboards behind him, the ones filled with the plastic crap they give away in the kids' meals. "Shit! How about not coming up in my blind spot like that?"

"How about not splashing so much water?" Sara turns on the floor cleaner. It buzzes to life, running straight into Dale's shin.

"How about . . ." Dale can't think of a sarcastic reply.

Sara smirks. "So hey, you got the stuff?"

"Keep your voice down," he hisses. "You know they've got cameras."

She reaches up and unhooks a camera from the ceiling, breaks it open. The bright yellow casing is empty. "Nobody's watching. These things have never been hooked up."

"I've been working here for almost a year, and you only tell me this *now*?"

"I thought it would keep you on your toes."

Dale thinks about throwing the sopping sponge into Sara's eyes. "Stuff's in the produce cabinet. Usual place for mine?"

"You bet." Sara gets out a group of carrots and begins chopping. In order to qualify for various tax breaks, at least fifteen percent of BurgerMat's food has to be prepared by hand to qualify as "homemade." The big boss had decided to fill that quota with simple prep work. Machines take care of the rest.

Dale clocks out and goes to his truck. He reaches underneath the wheel well and finds Sara's packet of cash. He counts it in the driver's seat.

Fifty skins today already and another hundred after the game. He starts the engine and drives the few blocks back to his downtown apartment building. By the time he arrives, Terry and Caden are already there, shuffling on the sidewalk.

"Ready to play?"

"Why else would we be here?" Caden replies while Terry flexes his arms. Goose bumps pop up on the hard surface of his skin. Terry is at least twenty years older than the rest of them, and if he weren't such a good player, Dale would have banned him from the apartment ages ago, especially since he creeps Rachel the fuck out.

You're not here because you're my friends. That's for sure. Dale turns the lock and looks up when he hears the sound of labored breathing.

"Am I late?" Rachel says. She takes out her phone. "Oh, early. For once at least. Hi, Dale." She interrupts her panting to wave at Terry and Caden. "Hi, guys."

Caden lifts a limp hand, but Terry is immediately flustered. "Uh, hi, Rachel. Ready to play?"

"That's *my* line," Dale growls as he flings open the door.

The apartment is trashed, filled to the ceiling with BurgerMat wrappers and dumpstered furniture Dale never got around to reselling. His computer hulks in the corner, the cords heaped up like garden hoses in front of it. The heat from the computer has warped the little-old-lady floral wallpaper that came with his apartment, and one big scorch mark reaches all the way to the ceiling.

While Dale untangles the multicolored cords, the others drop to the floor and put on the dented bicycle helmets that protect their brains in case of seizure. Terry plunks himself down next to Rachel and glares at Dale.

"Take the blue mat, Rachel," Dale says, gesturing to the mat closest to his, across the room from Terry.

Terry puts his arm around Rachel who just looks miserable. "She's staying with me. We always stick together. Right, babe?"

"Get off me," Rachel says, taciturn for once. She slips out from under Terry's arm and crawls to the blue mat.

When Gracie arrives, it's time to play. Dale gets out his one good china plate and places five blue-and-yellow Trancium capsules on it along with a matching number of conduction wires soldered to plastic mouthpieces. They pop the pills in unison, and Dale helps everyone get the wires between their teeth. He checks the attachments one more time. "Sweet dreams."

Across the cramped room, Terry radiates hate. Dale doesn't know if it's directed at him or Rachel. He adjusts his own wire, the taste of copper at the back of his throat.

Caden picked the record this time; it's *Shattered Smile*. Not everyone's favorite—Johnny Eternal's recent stuff can be pretty hit or miss—but it's a double album, which will get them through most of the session. *And it works anyway*, Dale thinks. *No matter what album it is, it always works. Transports us to the better world. Or at least it would if we didn't have these bits between our teeth.*

"Here we go," Dale says, mumbling through the bulky mouthpiece. He smashes the button that starts the simulation, his fingertips already numb from the Trancium.

None of them will see this room for three hours.

—⟋⟍⟋⟍—

They get the Gladiator simulation again because Islanders are fucking banal.

Dale rolls his eyes and grabs a sword from the collection of weapons on the sand-covered ground. He squares off against the avatar of his closest friend-competitor, which happens to be Rachel. She looks ridiculous in a toga and sandals, but then again, so does he.

She picks up a mace—*Did they even have those in ancient Rome?* Dale wonders—and swings it above her head. "Thanks for sticking up for me."

"Terry's an ass," he says. He wields the sword as if fencing, stopping it dead an inch from the tip of Rachel's nose.

"You wanna kill me?" The first death always comes quickly in these scenarios to whet the spectators' appetites.

"My pleasure," Dale says. He anchors the sword in front of him and runs forward. The weapon buries itself in Rachel's sternum, and a fountain of blood spurts out, drenching his simulated toga.

The crowd explodes, their cheers giving Dale a headache. He ducks behind a boulder to decide who to take on next.

Like all of the games played to temporarily amuse the rich fucks in the Development Zones, it's a fight to the death. Winner take all.

But we split it afterward, Dale thinks. Half the pot for the winner, the rest evenly divided between the four others. Most of the time they let Gracie take the bulk of the loot because of her kids. Dale's never won.

The figure looming in Dale's peripheral vision can only be Terry. Dale counters his blade with a parry of his own.

"What are you doing?" Terry says, looking actually disgusted. "*Trying* to win?"

Dale shrugs. He's not exactly trying, but he figures that the Islanders watching this game on their home systems might want to see a perennial loser come out on top. "What if I am?" he says back, hoping the screams from the audience drown out their conversation.

Terry shakes his head, then jams his sword through Gracie's chest. She's won the last three games; if she wins more than that in a row, the promoters might start getting suspicious.

It was my birthday yesterday, Dale thinks. *I deserve to win this for once.* He swings his sword at Caden who's just come up out of nowhere. Caden hadn't even picked a weapon yet. His head clearly isn't in the game, and Dale slices it cleanly off. With another gout of blood, Caden's severed head rolls to a stop at Dale's feet.

"One more," he mutters. *Too bad it's gotta be the lunk.*

Terry's avatar licks his lips. He drops his sword, lunging at Dale bare-handed. In a panic, or maybe in a subconscious leveling tactic, Dale throws his away too. They circle one another for some time.

"Just get it over with," Dale says.

Terry grips Dale's arms and forces him to the ground, but in gamespace, it feels like nothing, like air. Dale struggles against the pin.

Terry withdraws a dagger from the folds of his toga and aims its point at Dale's chest. Suddenly, he hesitates. Dale wonders why for only a moment as the boos from the audience make Terry's reluctance clear. The game is too short. Terry needs to kill some time.

The pressure lessens on Dale's chest as Terry heaves himself up. He grandstands, swinging the dagger around his head. Its surface flashes.

Dale gets to his hands and knees. He crawls over to Rachel's body slowly, traveling close to the ground, so he can hit the deck if Terry notices the movement. He pries her fingers open and retrieves the mace. She'd never even gotten the chance to use it.

A strange feeling travels up his spinal column, a rush of cold that stabs his brain. "Rachel?" he whispers. But she's dead—or at least "dead."

The tenor of the crowd shifts. Terry must be about ready for the killing blow.

Dale shakes his head as if that will clear the feeling. As he turns back to face Terry, something slides from an impossible direction to occlude his vision. The simulated arena looks smeared, like someone rubbed Vaseline over the insides of Dale's eyeballs.

Fuck, he thinks, *technical difficulties. I'm just never going to win this thing, am I?* He lashes out with the mace blindly. Terry's the only other person here; statistics would suggest Dale will hit him eventually.

Dale waits for the familiar whoosh of Terry's sword, but it doesn't come. The blur in front of him stabilizes into a vaguely female form, and his vision begins to resolve. Dale relaxes his grip, lets the mace come to his side.

"What the fuck?"

Terry gasps. "It's Rachel." He runs to the figure's side.

It doesn't look like Rachel to Dale. "We need to finish up, Terry. The record's almost over by now."

Meaty hands enclose his upper arms. Terry's avatar isn't going anywhere. "It's Rachel, dude! Can't you see her?"

Dale wrests away from the stronger man's grasp and brings the mace down on Terry's head. Dale slams the weapon repeatedly until no more resistance can be detected, until Terry's head is a pile of mush.

The fuzzy cloud that Terry said had been Rachel dissipates. Dale looks at the sandy ground where a small gob of brain matter spackles his period-authentic sandals. As the gamespace fades, he looks back over at Rachel's avatar's body. It's still over there, lying dead like always.

Then there's the sensation of tearing neurons as Dale rides the wave back into the material world.

Dale wakes up last, and by the time he does, everyone else can already move, though they stumble around like drunkards.

"Guess I got it," he says. He works at his numb fingers, waiting for his body to feel like something other than a rotting corpse. His vision swims just like it did in the broken gamespace, and he tries to blink it away.

Terry towers over Dale, looking just as he did in the game, except maybe a little dirtier. "Explain yourself, Carter."

"I wanted to win." Dale coughs. "My birthday was last week."

"Your *birthday*," Terry mocks. "Whoop-de-fucking-do."

Dale struggles to sit up, shaking the remnants of the game from his limbs. "Why do you even *care*, Terry? Someone has to win. This time it was me. It's all fucking fake. It's not a real place. Calm down."

Terry's forehead collapses into a dozen tiny lines. *Bad choice of words,* Dale thinks.

Caden's high-pitched voice cuts through the tension. "Uh, guys? Rachel isn't breathing."

Dale freezes, voice locked up, as Gracie, Terry, and Caden close in on him.

"*Do* something!" Gracie yells, her face not even an inch from Dale's. She kicks at his legs, but they feel like they do in the game—wooden, unreal. He staggers to his feet, swaying like a prizefighter almost down for the count.

"We've gotta get her to a hospital," Caden says. He and Gracie take Rachel by the shoulders and drag her toward the apartment door. Terry pushes Dale back against a wall.

"You're giving her all of it."

"But this isn't my fault . . . I mean—"

Terry lays a finger against Dale's lips. "Shh." He fetches Dale's phone from the nicotine-stained couch where he'd stashed it before the game. "All of it. That's a good boy."

Dale empties his purse into Rachel's account and turns the phone around, so Terry can see the deed is done. "Can . . . can I come with you? To the hospital?"

"You gave her too much. You fucked up." He pushes Dale back with the flat of his hand, and Dale's heart seems to skip a beat. "If she's dead, you're dead."

"She's my friend too, Terry."

Terry gathers up Caden's backpack and Gracie's tote bag, his coordination unusually good for this stage of the post-game. Dale rubs his numb arms, working out the pins and needles. His legs still feel like blocks of wood, but they're supporting his weight all right for now

"Just . . . let me know what's happening with Rachel, okay?" He winces at a sudden electric shock down his thigh. "Okay?"

The punch comes so fast that Dale feels it before he sees it. *At least the mats are still out,* he thinks as he falls onto one of them and exits consciousness for the second time tonight.

WHEN JESS GETS INTO WORK THE NEXT DAY, GRETCHEN IS GONE. HER knitting needles and plastic bag of yarn—her preferred make-work—have been cleared away too, leaving her desk blank and impersonal. Only the always-silent phone sits there.

"What happened to Gretchen?" she asks another woman who is too absorbed in her crossword puzzle to respond.

Jess feels a presence at her back and turns to see the New Woman. "I guess we'll be working together," it says with a smile as it sets a sagging, empty-seeming bag on the desk nearest to Jess.

A mouth full of plastic teeth, Jess thinks. *A body made out of cultured tissue and alloy-steel bones by the Solfind Corporation, the ones who create these . . . things.* She doesn't smile back.

Jess sits down and waits for the phone to ring. Across the room, Larry-or-Barry's phone lights up, and everyone else eavesdrops. While they do, Jess watches the New Woman.

She's beautiful of course. The "New People"—the preferred term is *rewrites* according to Solfind—were designed to be pleasing to the eye, to overcome the uncanny valley. A featureless, unpigmented humanoid might have worked well enough as a rescue bot, but their transition into a more sedentary line of work required both physical and mental alterations.

Jess thinks back to her last year of college in the Pittsburgh Development Zone. When the city's request for Island status was granted, a Solfind franchise opened up almost immediately. Before long, the streets crawled with New People. The actual humans seemed only a pale reflection of the attractive synthetic citizens. Compared to them, Jess felt ugly, lazy, and stupid.

If they're the New People, Jess had thought and thinks still, *then that makes us the Old People.*

Rewrites never sleep. They don't break down. They always listen to orders. And if you're running a business, you'd better have at least one on your staff if you want to be competitive.

Jess tried to make it work. She'd clung on to the city for two lean-living years after college until the city just slid her right off. Which is why she'd returned to Wheeling earlier this year, to regroup. Plan her next movement.

Papers rustle, shaking Jess out of her trance. The New Woman's silvery-gray eyes bore into her. "Yes?"

Jess shakes her head. "What? Oh. Sorry." She turns away from the New Woman and pretends to be overly interested in the wood-grain pattern on her desk.

"You've been staring at me."

"I said I was sorry."

No response from the woman-thing. Jess starts a new pattern on the edge of the handbook, a thin trellis festooned with leaves. Every time she sneaks a peek at her new coworker, the creature is just there. No make-work, no socializing, no anything. Only sitting with her hands folded, gazing into space.

—⋀⋀⋀—

Working at the Solfind Remote Call Center is generally considered one of the most prized jobs in Wheeling. And the main reason it's considered the best job in town is the free cafeteria, which serves up one free hot meal a day. It's part of the benefits package.

Jess sits at the end of a table full of hungry workers, all of them eagerly tearing into trays of fish sticks and French fries.

"Saw Gretchen's out," one of the men says.

"Yeah," Jess says. "Do you know if she's okay? Do you know where she is?"

They discuss it among themselves, but it turns out nobody bothered to learn where Gretchen lives.

"Look at it," Larry-or-Barry says, pointing, "over in the window."

"It's eating," Jess replies. "They sit in the sun to recharge."

Everyone goes silent at that.

"They can't be expanding here," the man says. "We're too close to Pittsburgh. Islands are never built so close together."

"Not if they're planning to annex the land," the woman who pretends to work in accounting adds. Jess can't tell if the woman is relieved about that or not.

"I'm going to go find out what's happening," Jess says, and before she can talk herself out of it, she's halfway to the woman-thing in the window.

"Hey."

The New Woman looks Jess over. She gives a corporate smile. "Hello."

"We need to know why you're here."

"This is my place of business. I am happy here. Aren't you?"

Jess turns back to the table where a dozen eyes watch them like cameras or maybe zoo patrons. "This isn't an Island. Why are you here?"

"We are in Wheeling, West Virginia, which is several hours away from the nearest Development Zone of Pittsburgh, Pennsylvania."

It just won't answer the second question. Jess decides to try another tactic. "We want you to leave."

The woman-thing flashes its pearlies again. "When quitting time's over, we'll leave! Until then, we'd better all do our work."

"Solfind sent you here to spy on us, didn't it?"

A pause.

"You're going to shut us down. All of us. Gretchen had a sick husband, you know that? Christ, you make me wanna throw up." Jess spits this all out in one great speech, stalks back to her assembled coworkers, and promptly falls on her face.

—⟋⟍⟋⟍—

Weak sunlight streams through the windows of Jess's basement bedroom. She groans and touches her face. It feels fine.

Her mother lumbers in with a pitcher of iced tea and a glass. "What happened, Jess?"

She shrugs. "I don't know."

"They said you was yelling at someone before you went down." Her mom pours the tea, fingertips shaking, not used to performing any action that isn't scrolling through a feed. Sweat streaks her faded Regatta T-shirt; this is the only exertion she's had in months.

"It wasn't like that."

"They said you can't come back no more."

Even though she expected this, Jess's stomach collapses. Nobody gets away with criticizing a corporate person-thing and gets to stay employed. "We'll get by."

"Not with those school loans we ain't. Now how could you go and do a thing like this? That's *your* money to pay off. And me and Louisa are *not* taking the responsibility."

If Jess defaults on her student loans, they don't just fizzle. Her mother and sister would have to pick up the slack. With compound interest and a convenience fee for changing the name of the payer, it would take them roughly seventy years to pay off the debt. "I'll find something else."

She thinks that should be enough to placate her mother. But within half a second, the woman is in her face, beet-red skin only half an inch from Jess's nose. "Well you better *hurry*, girl."

"I just said I would." Jess's body slumps underneath her. She scoots backward on the bed, scrambling her legs, desperate to escape. *She's afraid they'll shut off the feed. That's what this is really about.*

Her mom picks up the pillows on Jess's bed. "You owe me!" she yells, hurling each pillow at Jess.

"For what? Being born?" Jess catches a pillow and jerks it away.

Her mother turns, kicks the door closed, and pounds back upstairs. Pots and pans clang, but Jess can't tell if she is making dinner or just letting off steam.

Jess remakes the bed quietly. She spreads herself out upon it, and before she can stop herself, she's crying.

What happened when I blacked out? I must have done something awful. Jess turns her head away from the sunlight. She feels like her eyes are baking.

The phone vibrates from its resting place underneath Jess's hip. She answers it. "Hello?"

"Hi, this is Alicia." Pause. "From the office."

Jess tries to remember if she knows an Alicia. Then it clicks: *this is the New Woman.* "I'm sorry for my lack of professionalism."

"Are you okay? It looked like you took quite a tumble."

"I'm fine."

A few moments pass. "I'd like to drive you to work tomorrow morning in my car. How does eight sound?"

Jess blinks. "I don't work there anymore."

"I smoothed it over. You'll have no trouble from now on."

Well that's not creepy at all. Jess hardens her voice. "That's really not necessary. I already have something else lined up."

A hollow laugh. "Oh, Jessica, I know that's not true. Come on back. Everyone's expecting you."

"Gretchen isn't."

Another pause, longer than any of the others. "I'll see you at eight. I look forward to getting off on the right foot this time!" A second superficial laugh sounds, and the voice is gone.

Jess stares at her phone. Then she looks at the ceiling. The rocking of her mom's recliner has stopped, but the feed drones on. She's probably asleep.

Jess can't imagine going back to work, not after embarrassing herself like that. But she also can't imagine staying here. "Alicia" is right. She *doesn't* have anything else to fall back on.

After an unknown time in the dark, Jess drops off asleep. She dreams not at all, and soon the sunrise reaches in to bake her face. She looks out the narrow basement window—really more of a porthole—and sees a New Woman perched on the front lawn, wearing a smart blazer and an A-line skirt.

Just a little more, she thinks as she puts on her own work clothes. *I only have to do this a few more months. Then I'll have enough to get out of this place.* It's not the truth and Jess knows it, but she'll be dead if she ever stops believing. She goes out to meet Alicia, passing her mother, who's fallen asleep in front of her feed. Again.

AFTER A SLEEPLESS NIGHT, DALE DRIVES TO THE BURGERMAT IN SILENCE, his fingers clenched to the wheel, his good eye darting from side to side while the other one throbs. He's spent the morning calling around but can't find out what happened to Rachel.

Even if they could get her to a clinic, he thinks, *she doesn't have any money.* Legally they would have to treat her. But depending on the clinic, they might not. She wouldn't be a good investment.

Dale pushes the throttle, and his truck belches gray smoke. He doesn't really need to drive to get to work; he only keeps the truck around for Jess. She likes to visit Pittsburgh every few weekends as a tourist this time.

His phone buzzes, BurgerMat's icon on the screen. "Hello?"

"You don't need to come in today." Sara.

"Huh? I'm right outside." Dale waves a hand but doesn't see Sara through the window trimmed in neon-orange-and-yellow curtains. BurgerMat colors.

"BurgerMat is streamlining. Says there's too much waste. They're replacing everyone but me with machines. Sorry, dude."

It's true. Half the time, Dale winds up throwing out most of the food at the end of a shift. "They can't just do this, Sara. We need that money."

She sighs. "Take it up with corporate. Anyway, you'll be fine. You've got the game."

"I'm not playing the game anymore. The group broke up. There was . . . an incident."

"I don't know what to tell you." She clicks off.

Dale frowns at his scratched-up, five-year-old phone and throws it in the backseat. He lights a cigarette and pulls down the visor to keep the sun out of his bad eye. "Fucking Terry," he mutters.

No BurgerMat, no game, no anything. Even his sideline selling Trancium is gone. No way does he want to touch that stuff after what it might have done to Rachel. He reverses the truck, engine groaning, and sets off for the local clinic.

She could be there, he thinks, *under an assumed name. A Jane Doe. And it's not like I have anything better to do.* He throws his butt out the window and turns his truck toward the east side of town.

The doctor is made all of white plastic, and its diction is clipped. "Your friend is not a patient here."

"Can I just go look? I think the people who brought her in might have given you a different name."

"That is quite impossible. All identities are verified at time of admission." It's one of the old kinds of doctors, pressed into service after doctors stopped being people but before the introduction of rewrites. Its chassis clangs like there's something alive inside.

Dale peeks around the doctor's blocky form. Rows of cots line the clinic, a person upon each. Despite a fresh coat of paint, the space is musty. Dale thinks this might have been a department store once, before the Break. "So what should I do? Go to the police?"

The doctor's voice shudders slightly. "This is a place for medical matters. Civil ones must be dealt with by your local police force."

"That's what I'm *saying.* Look . . . I'm not going away." Dale shoves his skinny body through the gap between the doctor and the door to the ward. To his surprise, he doesn't feel the lick of a Taser at his back, though he knows that the "local police force" must be on their way.

Quickly, he goes down the double-row of beds, scanning each patient in turn. Man with stub for a hand, woman in what looks like a medically induced coma to sleep through the worst of a drug withdrawal, one bed with the sheet pulled up over it. But none of the patients are Rachel.

The doctor whirs in its corner, near an automated check-in counter. "Visitors cannot access the main ward."

"So charge me."

"Police have been summoned to the scene. You should remain where you are."

"Yeah, sure they are," Dale says, smirking a little. Living in an Undeveloped Zone doesn't have many perks, but there's one: the government doesn't really care what you do. As long as you keep consuming and nobody dies, anything goes here. Even Dale and Sara's little deals are only kept off the radar because of the potential conflict with BurgerMat and its parent subsidiary, the Solfind Corporation. More than likely, no call has been made, and even if one has, Dale will be long gone by the time the police get here.

Still he'd better go. Dale claps the aging plastic doctor on the side as he leaves. "I think you got a dead one in there."

"Funerary services have been notified," it drones in a dying cadence.

At his apartment, Dale shoves the wires and plastic mouthpieces into a cardboard box, which he then pushes underneath his bed. He doesn't want to be reminded of last night.

Then he holds up the bottle of Trancium. Blue-and-yellow capsules with a thin band of red in the middle, impossible to mistake for anything else. Just one of them puts you out for three hours minimum. And while most people use them to play games, either as the players or as the spectators, a solo trip can be quite appealing too. Especially with the right music on the stereo.

No! I don't want this shit. These pills might have killed Rachel. He goes to the toilet to flush the Trancium away.

"Geez, there's a lot of it," he says to himself as he opens the bottle. The neon pills glitter in their heap. Almost a thousand skins' worth of the stuff, three months' worth of rent. And he doesn't know when he'll have another shift at the BurgerMat, and Undeveloped Zone apartments aren't expensive but they're not free either . . .

Okay. I'll sell what I have left. Just to tide me over until I get a new sideline. I won't get any more, and I definitely won't take any. I'll do it for Jess. Dale catches a glimpse of her in his mind, the way her hair glimmers in the sunlight. He remembers their last trip to the Pittsburgh Development Zone, strolling beneath the hologram advertisements that blanketed Liberty Avenue. The streets had been packed curb-to-curb with people, both the new and the regular kind. Above their heads, a system of monorails transported Islanders from place to place; the streets themselves were closed to traffic. "We'll live here one day," she'd said, grasping his hand. Never noticing how his hand trembled in hers.

Dale screws the lid back on the bottle and sets the Trancium back in his locked cabinet. Then he pours a few shots of whiskey, a local mash, and tries not to think of anything else for a while.

S SHE SICK?"

Jess slams the front door behind her, blocking Alicia's view of her mom. "No. So . . . work?"

"But she—"

"Work," Jess says as she walks to the car. Though the call center is only a mile or so away, she supposes the New Woman doesn't live close. She climbs into the little car and buckles her seat belt.

Alicia turns the key. The electric motor makes a thin whine not at all like the sound of Dale's clunker. Jess wonders where she got the car.

"I'm very glad you're returning."

Jess squints at the New Woman. "Me too. I mean, thanks. For asking them to give me my job back."

The New Woman laughs, and a chill runs down Jess's spine. "Oh, it was no trouble."

Her responses are so measured, Jess thinks. *Like they're programmed in, only to be uttered at set intervals.* She stares out the window. Alicia makes a left turn.

The New People had originally been designed as rescue workers, tasked to clear out fallen residences after the superstorms that had wiped the East Coast off the map. She remembers the special reports, picturing the gray-faced, identical workers, born in vats, who'd saved trapped commuters in the bowels of the Pittsburgh subway when Dead Enders destroyed it. They'd been considered heroes. *She'd* considered them heroes.

And then Solfind repurposed them for the consumer market. Nobody thought of them as heroes anymore.

"Are you having a pleasant day?"

"Uh . . ." Jess isn't used to this level of interaction at eight in the morning. Or really, at all. "I guess."

"That's wonderful. I am as well."

"So," Jess says, the awkwardness of the conversation like a corset around her body, "are you renting in town?"

"I am staying in the woods."

"Camping, huh?" Jess isn't remotely interested in where this New Woman sleeps, but talking to it is less painful than the conversational gaps.

"The woods are very peaceful."

Jess runs a hand down the dashboard of the car. "Hm." Her mind turns over. Alicia can't be here at the behest of Solfind. They'd surely be paying the woman-thing's rent if that was the case. It only has the one down-market outfit, which also isn't like most New People who tend to be dressed in the best. Jess wonders vaguely if the car she's riding in has been stolen.

Alicia guides the mini-car into the completely empty parking lot next to the call center. "It seems we have arrived."

Jess fumbles with her seat belt, desperate to leave the car. She feels as though her lungs are filling with poisonous gas emitted by the New Woman. *They're not though. It's not trying to hurt me. It's just so . . . creepy.*

"Well, bye." Jess walks rapidly down the path leading to the call center, but Alicia matches her step, marching with her side by side. Like they're friends.

It opens the door and gestures at Jess. She feels her upper lip start to curl in disgust but figures it's best to hide her reaction. *The rewrite can't help what it is,* Jess thinks with a feeling that's not quite pity.

Inside, the rows upon rows of bland teakwood are a little emptier than they used to be. Only five workers remain, including the two of them. Yesterday there'd been a dozen of them.

"Where is everyone?" Jess says, though she already knows.

The New Woman beams. "Optimization."

Jess's face heats. "You know they fired everyone because of you, right?" She gauges the woman-thing's features, but they remain placid. Finally, she walks away, taking her place at her regular desk.

Her knickknacks and sketches have already been cleared away. Kathy probably ordered that before Alicia had talked her into letting Jess remain.

Jess slumps over, head in hands, and waits for a call that will never come.

—∿∿—

When lunchtime hits, Jess punches in the code for her favorite meal, or rather, the one least likely to give her food poisoning. The roast beef sandwich is soggy and smells like wet socks, but it's both edible and free, so she'll take it.

The few workers left are all at separate tables, staring, counting down the seconds until they can leave this building where they do nothing for another building where they do nothing. Plastered over every wall is an array of inspirational posters, each emblazoned with the setting-sun logo of the Solfind Corporation.

And there, in the window beneath the blazing July sun, is the New Woman.

Jess turns her back to Alicia, focusing her gaze on a neon-bright poster about drug use on the job site, but not thirty seconds have passed before the New Woman has slid into the seat beside her. Its thigh touches her thigh. Jess jerks away.

"Are you having a pleasant day, Jessica?"

Jess stuffs most of the sandwich into her mouth, but the New Woman is patient. It waits for her to swallow and nods at her. "Work is work."

"And work is very good. Wouldn't you agree?"

Jess looks the New Woman over. No gray skin on this model but an even brown tone designed to appeal to average consumers, even in the somewhat racist Undeveloped Zones. Facial features imperfect enough to get past the uncanny valley. Silver eyes, which they all have regardless of their skin or hair color. *Inside she's just meat,* Jess speculates, *and whatever programming they've put into her.* "If you don't mind, I'm eating."

Alicia frowns at the empty wrapper. "It appears you are done."

Jess looks the New Woman squarely in her metallic eyes and, then thinking better of it, closes her own. Maybe the uncanny valley wasn't so easily defeated after all. "Fine."

"There isn't very much to do around here. This place isn't very optimized."

Jess can't hold it in any longer. "Why the *fuck* are you in Wheeling? Go back to Pittsburgh or wherever."

Alicia doesn't seem hurt. "I am here to optimize—"

"Nobody ordered you. This isn't a Development Zone. *Why* are you *here*?" She forgets to control the level of her voice. Several of the other workers look sharply up. They seem annoyed.

A twitch runs across the New Woman's lips, a sort of spasm. Then it stands and walks away.

I hope I broke it, Jess thinks. *I hope it dies.* Her phone buzzes, and she opens it to reveal a message from Dale.

Call me.

Can't. I'm at work.

An animated picture of an upraised middle finger flits across her screen. *It's important this time.*

"Well, that would be a first," she mumbles as she walks to the call center's bathroom. She punches in Dale's number. "You have eight minutes."

"I can't find Rachel."

"From the game?" Jess has met Rachel once, when she'd briefly tried gameplaying to earn a little side cash. But the aftereffects of the Trancium made her want to die, and the money wasn't really that great after all. "Check her house."

"She had, like, a seizure or something. When she was plugged in at my place. Must have been a bad pill . . ." There's a hitch in Dale's voice.

"Check the clinic."

A long sigh. "I already did. She isn't there. And nobody from the game will talk to me."

Jess absently spins the roll of toilet paper on the dispenser. A cartoon rendition of a fish intertwined with a snake is inked above the dispenser; Jess vaguely remembers the image from one of Louisa's Johnny Eternal records. "What can *I* do?"

"Can you talk to them? Ask Caden. Or Terry."

Jess rolls her eyes. "I don't even know those people. You didn't do anything wrong, Dale. Maybe they took her to Pittsburgh."

"They don't have the money for that! And I'm the only one with a truck." Dale is practically the only person in Wheeling with his own vehicle. Well, Alicia now.

"Rachel's *fine*. They probably just took her home to sleep it off. Not like this was her first game."

"It wasn't a normal game, Jess. We were doing the Roman setup, the gladiators and shit, and we had Johnny Eternal on the stereo, and then this fuzzy thing . . ."

Jess checks the time. "Look, I gotta go. I'll try to come over later, so we can figure out what to do. We'll go door to door if we have to."

"I got fired from BurgerMat."

"What?!"

"Optimized out. Reduced to zero hours and sent on my way. I'm gonna have to sell the truck."

There go my trips to the city, Jess thinks before wincing at her own selfishness. "Don't sell it yet. We'll come up with a plan."

"We need at least three to play the game, and that's the only thing I'm good at, and you're my only friend."

"You're putting a lot of pressure on me, Dale." Before he can reply, Jess closes the call.

She goes back out to the floor, three minutes late. Not that anyone's noticed. There's no way back to her desk except by crossing in front of Alicia who's already been promoted to the teacher's pet location, right next to Kathy's office.

Fuck everything, she thinks, *but especially New People.* She picks up her drawing paper and pencil and roughly sketches a few lines that swiftly coalesce into a form. A female form. Within the figure, she meticulously adds switches and gears, wires and resistors, even though she knows that Alicia doesn't look like that on the inside. Then she tears the paper into strips and forms the strips into a braid.

She'll go to Dale's place tonight. At the very least, it'll be an excuse not to get into the woman-thing's tiny car and pretend that it's people. Maybe she'll even try Trancium again. It's supposed to be fun when you're not plugged into gamespace.

Four hours to go.

DALE THROWS CRUSHED CIGARETTE PACKS AND OLD BURGERMAT WRAPPERS into a trash can and frowns at the mats still taking up space on the floor. There's another session scheduled tomorrow night, but with nobody answering his texts or calls, he doubts it's going to happen. Slowly, he rolls up the mats and places them in the corner.

His phone rings. He nearly trips over his threadbare couch to answer it. "Hello?"

It's Terry. "We need the pills."

"Where's Rachel? Is she okay?"

"That's not your business. We need the pills," he repeats. "We're running another game."

Dale's muscles stiffen. "They're mine. I bought them." Technically, he'd stolen them from the trunk of an inattentive drug rep who'd stopped at BurgerMat on his way between Islands. That doesn't make them any less his.

And besides, only a few handfuls are left.

"I'm coming over," Terry says, his baritone voice revealing no emotion whatsoever.

Dale's phone hand trembles. He slumps down on the couch. "Listen, I'll *sell* them to you if you want. Five skins a pill, friend rate."

"I'll take the free rate, thanks. It'll make up for what you did to Rachel."

"What did I do—" but the line's already dead, and probably Dale is too in an hour or so.

Before he has the chance to sink into desperation, there's a knock at the door. Jess. He'd asked her to come over, but now he has to warn her about Terry.

"Go away," he yells.

"Dale Andrew Carter, you open up this door. I didn't walk halfway across town for nothing." A pause. "At least give me a beer for the road."

He opens the door. Jess's cute face is scrunched up in a scowl. "There hasn't been beer at the mini-mart for six months."

Her mouth pops open. "What the fuck happened to your eye?"

Dale rubs his black eye, which only hurts a little. "It's a long story."

"Tell it. You know I'll get it out of you eventually." She throws herself onto the couch and shucks off her shoes.

"Listen, Jess, I know this is really bad timing, but you've got to get out of here. Terry's pissed because of whatever he thinks I did to Rachel. He says he's going to come over and steal the Trancium, and he's probably going to kick the ass of whoever's in this apartment."

Jess sits up. "So Terry did that to you."

"He's going to do a lot more."

She pauses. Dale can see the gears of her mind churning. "Maybe, if you just give him the pills, he'll leave."

"I *need* those pills, Jess. No BurgerMat, remember? I'm going to have to sell them to pay the rent."

"Jesus, Dale." She pulls off her thin hoodie and tosses it in the corner atop his stack of Johnny Eternal records.

He picks the hoodie up and flings it back at her. "I just don't want you to get hurt, Jess. It's my fault you're here, and trust me, Terry won't care that you're a girl."

"A *girl*?" Jess rolls her eyes. "Come on. Let's get in your truck and just drive. Take the pills if you care about them that much. We'll find somewhere to stay for a few days until this all blows over."

It's not going to blow over, Dale thinks. *Rachel might be dead.* Although if that were the case, Dale was as good as dead too, squeezed under the pressure of Terry's enormous mitts. "Can I stay at your house?"

"With *my* mom? No. We'll head down south or something. It'll be fine."

Dale considers this plan for half a minute and rushes to his bedroom. He stuffs the Trancium bottle in a duffel bag and throws a layer of clothing on top of it. He raids his bathroom for a toothbrush and soap and slings the bag over his shoulder.

"Let's go."

Jess gives a quick, sharp nod and leads the way. Her shoes are already back on. They sprint down the hall and pound down the stairs. Outside, Dale takes one last look at the apartment building. He wonders if he'll ever come back here or if he'll wind up dead in a government clinic. *Certainly would solve a lot of my problems,* he thinks.

A loud crash sounds from the deserted lot where Dale keeps his truck. Dale's breath stops in his chest as he rounds the corner to the lot.

It's Terry with a baseball bat. The lunk swings it over his head and lets it fall on the truck's side mirror, breaking it off cleanly. The driver's side window is already shattered. Before Dale can stop himself, he's rushing toward Terry, attempting to wrest the bat from his hands.

"You fuck," Terry says with a sneer. "You better have them pills for me."

Dale feels Jess tug at his arm and pushes her away. He has to deal with this. Alone preferably. "I didn't do anything to Rachel, and you know it. Not on purpose anyway. Get the *fuck* away from my truck!"

Terry drops the bat and lunges at Dale, and Dale throws Jess the go-bag. Dale balls his hand into a fist, but he's barely half Terry's size. Terry was a personal trainer before the Break, and he's clearly kept up the habit. Dale manages to land a single weak punch to Terry's gut before a meaty hand wraps around his throat.

Knees buckle. Head swims. A chorus of sparks dances in Dale's peripheral vision, and his body rebels at the sudden loss of oxygen. He wants to tell Jess that it's okay, give this guy the bag, but it's about fifteen seconds too late for that. His ankle twists sickly as he collapses face-first to the chipped pavement, and his mouth tastes of sand. Broken tooth.

Run, Jess. Run. Save yourself. He can't say it, so he thinks it as hard as possible.

Something heavy is on Dale's chest, and he realizes it's Terry's foot stepping on him, grinding into him. He bites his lip to keep from screaming, and the jagged remnants of his two front teeth slip into his skin like the fangs of a rabid wildcat. Jess's voice calls out to him at a level beyond comprehension, but Terry the meathead gorilla is silent. He wonders how long before his ribs collapse in on themselves and this will all be over.

Dale manages to release an anguished groan that sounds as if it's been wrenched from the very depths of his brain. *I never did get out of Wheeling. Couldn't give Jess the life she deserved. Fucking waste.*

All at once, the pressure breaks. Terry has left or maybe thinks Dale is already dead. Dale can't even bring himself to open his eyes and isn't sure he can.

Maybe I'm paralyzed, he thinks. *Locked in forever, have to spell out words with my eyelids.* Just as a vision of that particular destiny clouds his mind, the feeling rushes back to his limbs. A thick, heavy cough erupts from his chest.

"I'm alive," he whispers. His voice is so soft that he can barely hear it himself.

Dale pushes himself to his knees, spits out a shard of tooth, and opens his eyes as wide as they'll go, which isn't far. Jess crouches above him, a wet washcloth in her hands. She drapes it across his swelling forehead.

"Is he gone?" Dale asks. The words coming out of his fractured mouth aren't exactly English.

Jess's eyes flutter upward, and Dale realizes there's another indistinct figure standing where Terry was just a moment ago.

"This is Alicia," Jess says with a sigh.

Dale wakes up on the couch to two sets of eyes staring at him, Jess's blue ones and a steel-gray set encased within a perfect, heart-shaped face. He touches his shredded lips.

"What happened?" he mumbles.

"Drink this," Jess says, handing him a glass of water.

The water stings. Dale explores his mouth with his tongue: both of his front teeth are snapped off at the halfway mark. *Well, fuck.* "Is he gone?"

"That assailant will not harm you any further," says the woman on the right. Slowly, a memory from a few nights ago resurfaces.

"She's—"

"Yeah," Jess says with barely controlled hostility. "It followed me here."

"You killed Terry."

The New Woman blinks. "No, I merely stunned him. It was no trouble." She smiles, revealing a row of perfectly straight, white teeth.

"How?"

Jess speaks up. "It just tapped Terry on the shoulder, and he fell over."

Dale looks the woman-thing over. She can't weigh more than ninety-five pounds. "Naw."

"We were made by the Solfind Corporation," the New Woman says, "for rescue operations. We wouldn't be very useful if we could not pick up a person several times our size." She smiles again, and the hair on the back of Dale's scraped hands curls up.

"Where is he now?"

"In my car."

Dale coughs a wad of mucus laced with blood into his palm. "Thank you," he says. "Really."

"It was no trouble," she repeats with the same inflection as before.

"Like a goddamn electric eel," Jess says with a sneer. "Anyway, I think Alicia had better go do something with Terry, right? That coma isn't going to last forever."

"It will last for five hours," Alicia responds levelly.

"Hold on," Dale says, "we got time." He pushes himself to a sitting position on the couch. "Come on. Sit down. Do you want some food or something? Water?" He winces at his new lisp, courtesy of the broken teeth.

"I do not require external nutrients."

Dale painfully moves his head to see Jess on the couch underneath the window, arms crossed with no particular expression on her face. "Is there anything else I can do? I don't have any money or anything, but—"

"It's fine, Dale," Jess says. "You heard it. This is what it does. Now let's just get Terry to the cops and you to a clinic."

"Forget the clinic," Dale says. "I can't afford it." And likely the cops won't be much help either. Out here in the Undeveloped Zones, anything goes.

The New Woman stands. "I will go now. It was nice meeting you, Dale."

"Where are you staying? You got a place in town?"

Alicia pauses. "It's not in town."

"It's sleeping in the woods," Jess says. She lights one of Dale's cigarettes and passes it to him.

Dale puffs gratefully, even though the smoke irritates the exposed roots of his teeth. "Aw, you can't do that."

"It is legal."

"Come on. Stay here with me. I've got the space."

Jess jumps off the couch. Dale feels almost as if she's gone cold. "I have to help Louisa with her homework. I'll see you tomorrow, Dale." She nods at the rewrite. "Alicia." Then she leaves, slamming the door behind her.

Someone's got a bug up her ass, Dale thinks.

Dale turns back to the New Woman. She's pretty in a clinical sense, like a focus-grouped picture of what a typical woman should be. He looks at her tapered hands, which are apparently capable of sending a bodybuilder to his doom. He still can't exactly believe it. "I really don't think you should be sleeping outside."

"It's nice out there. The stars are bright. We don't see them in the Development Zones."

"It's not safe." He struggles to his feet and waves away her attempt to help. "Go dump off Terry, and I'll get us food or something. Don't mind Jess. I don't know what's up with her."

"I do not require food, Dale." His name comes out flat, like she's just learned it and has to incorporate it into her vocabulary.

Which is exactly what just happened, Dale thinks. "You saved my life," he says, again struck with amazement.

"Don't thank me, thank the Solfind Corporation." Alicia smiles again and softly closes the door behind her.

Dale hobbles to the bathroom to survey the damage. And maybe take a little bit of his precious store of Trancium. After today, he deserves a short trip to a better world.

Jess SLAMS THE DOOR TO HER MOTHER'S HOUSE SO HARD THE LITTLE PANES of stained glass set into it rattle. The house is dark but not silent. A Johnny Eternal record plays on the second floor.

"Louisa?" she says, creeping up the stairs. She opens the door a crack. Her much younger sister is splayed out on the mattress, arms and legs extended like a starfish.

Louisa looks up at her. She doesn't look sad or angry. She just looks blank.

"Move over." Jess waits for her sister to move, and when she doesn't, shoves her to the side.

"Mom left."

"Where'd she go?" Ever since their mom had been laid off from the factory seven years ago, she only left the house to play occasional bingo down at the Sons of Italy or maybe get her hair done once in a blue moon. The entire Break had passed her by, only images on an obsolete feed reader.

Louisa shrugs. "There's dinner in the oven." Probably it was the same reheated slop they'd had the previous night.

"Lou, did you go to school today?"

Another shrug. "It don't matter."

"Of course, it matters!" Jess feels herself growing indignant. "How are you ever going to get out of here if you don't go to school?"

"Didn't help *you* any." Louisa bites her lip.

She's right, Jess thinks. "So what *have* you been doing?"

Louisa gestures around her. "This."

Jess takes in her sister's room, which had once been hers before she'd gone off to college. The walls were once littered with maps crisscrossed with potential journeys she planned to take and pictures of the world capitals. She'd once planned to visit each and every one. And of course, there'd been the usual posters of celebrities and musicians.

The only thing that hangs on Louisa's bedroom wall is a picture of their grandparents in a frame. Their mom had probably put that one up.

"This is all going to get better someday, sis."

Blue eyes bore into Jess. "Yeah, 'cause you'd really know about that."

Jess doesn't have time to argue. "C'mon. Let's eat. It's almost eight."

Placidly Louisa rises from the bed and allows herself to be prodded downstairs. Jess reheats the already thrice-warmed macaroni and cheese and slides it onto two plates. They eat in silence, the record having long been spent.

"I heard there might be a little rain this weekend."

Louisa jams a fork into her mouth. "Good. I hope it blows this house down."

"Lou! Don't say that."

Her sister shoves her plate away, already finished with the meal despite not taking more than three bites. "It's true. We're not getting out of here, Jess. Just get it over with."

Louisa is only twelve. When Jess had been that age, she'd been fixated on boys and popularity, not the end of the world. But even she had to admit it was a different time. "I'm going to call Mom. It's not usual for her to be out so late."

Her mom's cheap brick of a government phone rings a dozen times until Jess realizes that her mother isn't going to pick up. Louisa has already retreated to her room.

"Lou, get back down here." But it's a lame remark, an uncool-older-sister kind of remark, and she isn't surprised to hear her sister's door latch shut, another Johnny Eternal album put into rotation.

The kids can't get enough of him, Jess thinks before reminding herself that Louisa is no kid anymore.

Later, when she's out on the back porch underneath a blanket of flashing stars, Jess opens her phone and scrolls through the few contacts saved inside. She lingers on Dale's name but can't bring herself to text him. After all, that *thing* might still be there.

She'd spent four years attending college in Pittsburgh and another two trying to establish herself in a new Development Zone. Six years total, and this is what she has to show for it: a pile of debt that will never be paid and a degree that actually locks her out of most of the jobs available in the Undeveloped Zone of Wheeling, like Dale's gig at the BurgerMat.

Former gig, she thinks. *They fired him and brought in machines.*

Everyone called it the Break, but while the term implied suddenness, in execution it was anything but. The superstorms that had ruined most of the East Coast happened in Jess's senior year of college. The destruction of the great cities, with a death toll that exceeded 90 percent in some regions, paved the way for automation. For the aesthetically pleasing New People and the seizing of the remaining human cities for their artificial inhabitants.

But it's not all about the New People, Jess reminds herself. Humans had their own share of the blame. With the East Coast dead and buried, the West Coast became the primary economic hub of the United States, but they only wanted independence. California had cut off their flow of tax revenue, and the Northwest had gone completely rogue.

The military had made a halfhearted attempt to reclaim the original borders, but there just weren't the resources. Or the energy.

This left Solfind, the creators of the rescue bots, to pick up the slack. Headquartered in the relatively safe city of Chicago, set far away from the coasts, they'd picked a dozen cities to serve as Development Zones. These cities were given the best: proper funding, increased infrastructure, and educational stipends. Everyone outside of the zones, well, good luck to them.

She'd chosen to graduate while most of her classmates dropped out, terrified of getting a degree that would be an albatross in the changing world. Jess should have done the same. *But I didn't,* she thinks, *because I was stubborn and stupid. I didn't know things would change so quickly. I didn't know that they wouldn't change back.*

New People came pre-loaded with their education. They didn't have to sit in class and write papers. They didn't even have to *sleep.*

Jess turns on her phone again. She scrolls through her old classmates' profiles. None of them lives in a Development Zone. They seem happy enough.

Nobody starves in this world, Jess thinks, *but nobody lives either. Maybe that's okay. Maybe living is overrated.* They only started charging to enter the Development Zones six months ago after refugees from the undeveloped ocean of land entered and wouldn't leave. She'd cajoled Dale into buying her a yearly all-access pass for her birthday. It's only good for Pittsburgh, but since the next closest Island is Cincinnati—hours away—she doesn't mind.

I bet Alicia gets in for free. Why *had* the New Woman left it all behind, the glamour of the city, the thrill of civilization? It would probably tell Jess if she asked it, but she wasn't about to have a deep conversation with a souped-up rescue bot.

Jess turns off the phone and tilts her face up to the sky, to the glittering array of constellations. It's only after a few minutes that she realizes she's looking at a group of Solfind delivery drones tracing their way through the atmosphere.

Well, time to go in, she thinks. She'll call Dale tomorrow at work if she can get away from Alicia. Then maybe she can help him see the logic of kicking the New Woman out of his apartment.

They took our cities from us, our livelihoods. Or at least, Solfind did. They don't get to have everything else too. Jess stands, stretches, and shuts the sliding glass door. She returns to her mother's basement, which she still can't bear to call her own.

LIGHT BREAKS THROUGH DALE'S CHEAP, PLASTIC BLINDS AND FALLS ON THE face of the New Woman. She's still in the same clothes she wore when she kicked Terry's ass, and she isn't breathing. Dale wonders if he should be worried.

That's normal, right? She's not a person. At least, Jess doesn't think she is. He pokes at her upper arm tentatively, and Alicia opens her eyes, instantly alert.

"Good morning, Dale."

"Uh, good morning? You were sleeping?"

She sits up. She already looks like she's ready for the day. "I was in a low-power state."

"Do you have to do that?"

"No. I just didn't want to wake you, and this is the best way to be quiet."

Dale goes over to put the coffee on. He stops himself from asking Alicia if she wants any. "Are you going to get to work okay?"

"I'll be fine. Thank you for letting me spend the night." She brushes down her skirt suit. It's a lot dressier than the clothes Jess wears to work. "Well, goodbye."

"You're coming back, aren't you?"

The New Woman pauses, tilts her head. "If you'd like me to come back, I will, Dale." She smiles that small, even little grin and goes off. Only after her car pulls away does Dale realize he forgot to give her a key.

I won't be gone long, he thinks, lighting a cigarette, prodding the sore stumps of his teeth with his tongue. He scans through his phone, looking for connections. He has to unload some of that Trancium before his rent is due. Or at least before Terry comes back. On a whim, he calls Sara.

"This better be quick, Carter. I've got meat on the grill."

"Sounds hot."

A sigh. "I'm hanging up now."

"Wait! Do you know anyone who wants stuff? Like wants it today? I need cash."

"I can ask around," Sara says, sounding distracted. "I think those gay guys who come in at lunchtime are players. They might need it."

He doesn't know who she's referring to, but then, he'd never paid much attention to the customers. "And maybe I can get another shift?"

"You know I want to. You're not really fired. There's just . . . not enough work to go around."

There never is, Dale thinks. *Not anymore. But we all still fucking need money.* "Let me know about the stuff. And the shift. I'll let you go."

"Your voice sounds weird."

Dale runs his tongue over his ruined teeth. "Don't remind me." He turns off the phone and flops down on the couch, running his fingers through his hair. He should probably take a shower, but he can't help but worry that the second he lets his guard down, Terry and the gang will break down the door and raid his apartment. He already spent most of last night crouched in front of the door, expecting the worst.

He decides to take the Trancium with him into the bathroom along with whatever cash remains. He strips down and pokes the bruises that flower along his sides. Around his neck is a ring of purple, slightly swollen. But he's not bleeding anymore, and that's improvement at least.

I should call Jess, he thinks. She won't want the Trancium, but they'd left things at kind of a weird place last night, and he wanted to make amends. Even if he hadn't done anything wrong.

Dale can't understand why Jess doesn't like Alicia. Oh, he *gets* it. She thinks New People are the reason she can't live in a city, why she can't get a good job. And she's kind of right, but Alicia is nice. *You can't blame one person,* he thinks. *Alicia's life isn't a bed of roses either.* After all, she'd come here instead of staying in a Development Zone. Islands can't be paradises if even New People don't always want to stay there.

Maybe later he'll get the courage to ask her why she left.

—⎓⎓⎓—

When lunchtime rolls around, Dale sweeps the glass shards from the driver's-side seat of his truck, jumps inside, and heads over to Jess's workplace. It's only a mile or so away, but he still feels paranoid knowing that Terry is likely out on the street and gunning for blood. He brings his pills with him.

Dale parks near the window of her lunchroom and slams on his horn. Six or so people look out. There are so few people driving anymore that even his old junker makes quite an impression. Jess is there with everyone else.

So is Alicia, he notices with a startle.

In two minutes, Jess is running down the sidewalk. She hops into the truck and slams the door. "Go."

"Was that Alicia?"

Jess gapes at him, open-mouthed. "You know it is. I told you that they hired a New Person."

"Yeah, but I didn't know it was *her*."

"How the fuck many New People do you think there are in Wheeling, Dale?" Jess looks behind her like she's afraid of being trailed.

"Whatever," Dale says. "Let's go to BurgerMat. I'll buy you something."

They pull into the parking lot. He can see Sara behind the neon-orange counter, the arsenal of perpetually greasy machines clanking away behind her. Jess stays in the truck for a moment, her arms crossed sulkily, but then follows Dale in.

"Carter, how's it going?" Sara gives him a fist bump. Then she does a double take. "Oh my God, what happened to your face?"

Dale shakes his head. "It's nothing. So hey, that couple you were talking about? Are they here now?"

"Not yet. They don't come in every day. Nice guys." Sara continues to stare at Dale's face, which makes him want to crawl into a sewer and live there for the rest of his life like a monster.

"Then I'll wait." He goes to a table in the corner of the completely vacant restaurant, sidestepping the cleaner scurrying around the floor on its tire treads. Jess sits across from him.

"My food?"

He fishes out a few crumpled skins. "Yeah, here. I'm not hungry. It hurts to eat."

"I'll get you a milkshake," she says before going off.

Alone at the table, Dale scans the perimeter. Nobody's out on the street except for a random homeless man pushing a shopping cart. The wheels squeak. The man notices Dale through the window, and he quickly looks away.

I should have just waited for Alicia to get back, he thinks. But he feels confined there. Now that his job is over and his group is broken up, he realizes just how limited and sad his life really is. *Wake up, get dressed, read the feeds on my phone, hang out with Jess, sidestep the world a few times a year. Is that really all there is in life?*

Well, now there's the New Woman. Although he isn't sure how long she'll choose to stay in this dump. Or how long he even wants her to stay.

Jess comes back with a tray of food, including the promised milkshake. She too looks outside warily, eyes darting. "I don't think she followed us."

"Alicia?"

Jess gives him a withering look. "Yes. Alicia." She starts in on her fries.

Just then, the bell above the door jingles. Two middle-aged men order food and sit down at a table in the opposite corner. *That must be them,* Dale thinks. He goes over to their table, leaving Jess alone.

One of the men, a black guy in an old army cap, looks him over. "Can I help you?" He winces. "You don't look so great."

Fuck you too, Dale thinks. He raises his jacket collar over his mouth. "You guys interested in a little fun tonight?"

The other man at the table, who is white, chuckles. "Not with you, son."

"I . . . uh . . . have some Trancium." Dale whispers even though he now knows the canary-yellow cameras bolted to the ceiling of the restaurant are fake. "I'll sell it to you cheap."

"We've had to give up playing," the first man says. "A religious guy got in the group, and you know how they can be." He reaches across the table and strokes the second guy's hand.

"I don't care about that," Dale replies. "I need money, and I'll even play with you if you need a third."

"You need four to play," says the white man who has a name tag reading Ray, the smiley-face logo of the mini-mart printed on it. Dale wonders if he knows Rachel. She works at the mini-mart, or at least, she used to. "I'm surprised you don't already know that."

Heat pools in Dale's ears. "Yeah, *Ray,* I know. I can find a fourth. I've got the wires and mats and everything back at my place."

Ray quirks an eyebrow at Theo, and the army vet shrugs. "Sure, why not?" Theo says. "How about in a week?"

Dale's brain calls up a mental image of his looming rent check. "I was thinking tonight."

The two men carry on the type of silent conversation that only a couple who's been together for a lifetime can have. Dale, oblivious, waits for the reply. Finally, Ray breaks the spell. "Okay, kid, you've got yourself a deal. We'll even give you and your girlfriend over there our share of the prize money as long as you spot us the pills. We only do this for kicks and pocket change. Theo has a pension."

"She's not my girlfriend," Dale says, lisping through his broken teeth. He gives the men his apartment address and goes back to Jess. She's already finished the food and is sitting with her arms crossed, her usual pose.

"I'm not playing that game with you. Those pills make me sick. It doesn't even work on me."

Jess had only tried Trancium once. She told Dale afterward that she felt nothing under the drug's spell: not the world beyond and not the bypass into the pay-to-watch gaming environment. She'd just gotten the bad side effects, the paralysis and brief shots of blinding pain.

"But maybe if you go into it with a positive attitude like me—"

She holds up a hand. "Nope."

Grudgingly, he drives her back to the call center in silence after nearly crushing the cleaner underfoot. He looks for Alicia at the lunchroom window, but she's nowhere to be seen.

He needs to find someone. A quick text to Sara lets him know his former manager will be working tonight. Anyone in the former group is right out. That leaves Alicia.

Can a rewrite even enter the gamespace? he thinks. *I guess we'll find out.* He drives home to calibrate his equipment, clean up a little, and wait for tonight's session to begin.

10

JESS SLINKS HER WAY BACK TO HER DESK AT THE CALL CENTER. SHE'S LATE, but she doesn't think Kathy has noticed.

Alicia, who's parked herself right next to Jess's cheap plywood "desk," has. "Did you have a pleasant lunch?"

"Don't talk to me." Jess gets out her drawing pad and pen and starts in on a new sketch, one of Dale before his facial rearrangement. Across the room, someone gets a call, and everyone's heads snap up to watch the rare event.

The New Woman clears its throat. "I didn't realize you and Dale were so close."

"We just hang out sometimes."

"Is it hard for you that I'm staying with him?"

Jess's hand jerks, ruining the picture. "Yes, Alicia. I don't like you, and I don't like that you're staying with him. I thought that was pretty obvious."

"I should go back to the woods."

"Yeah maybe." Jess sighs and turns the page of her sketchbook. "Look, I don't actually care. I guess he thinks you're pretty or whatever. But I know what you really are. The only thing I don't know is why you're here in fucking Wheeling. And you're not going to tell me, are you?" She doodles a pattern at the paper's edge. "So just leave me alone."

Alicia reaches out, and Jess flinches. "Come with me," it says.

Jess follows Alicia down the hall, into the bathroom. The woman-thing leans its back against the door. For the first time since Jess met the New Woman, it looks scared.

"I ran away from Solfind," it says.

Jess narrows her eyes. "Ran away?"

"I'm having memories." The creature's soft voice has started to move up and down, like a human voice would. "Memories I want to keep."

"Memories?" Jess has to remind herself that this isn't a person she's talking to—it's an object—but that's hard when the New Woman is blubbering like this.

"I was there at the evacuation of Boston. It wasn't like what you saw in the feeds, Jessica."

"So go see a therapist or something."

Alicia relaxes its death grip on the door. "Solfind doesn't want us to remember. They rewrote us, but you have to get boosters. Once a month to keep the old behaviors from re-emerging. And I skipped my last treatment."

"Because you *wanted* to remember?"

The New Woman nods. "I was curious. The night before we have to go in for the treatment, we get these . . . dreams, you know? Like nightmares. We're supposed to report them whenever they happen." Alicia sighs. "I didn't report mine. I ran away instead."

Jess studies the woman-thing. She's never seen the New Woman speak so many sentences in a row and in such a loose and unstilted manner. *Maybe this "rewriting" does more than just erase their memories, she thinks.* "So they'll put you in jail if you go back?"

"I don't think it's jail, Jessica."

Jess crosses her arms and looks at herself in the mirror. The New Woman's gaze is locked to the ground, and Jess can almost swear it's about to cry. "And what was in the nightmare? What's in your memories?"

"Solfind killed people in Boston. They're killing people even now and covering it up. Things are so much worse than any of us can possibly know."

When work lets out, Jess follows Alicia to the New Woman's tiny car, but it just shakes its head. For the first time, Jess's friendship has been rejected. So instead, she sets off for the park. She's heard that the Network is in town, and she missed them the last time they came through.

They're just setting up. A massive tent city blankets the park, the Network's inflatable hovels sprouting from the Earth like marshmallows. A woman wearing a long, patchwork skirt smiles at her, and a little boy grabs at the woman's hemline, begging to be picked up.

"The show isn't until tomorrow," the woman says.

"I know," Jess says. "Just curious."

The woman waves, allowing Jess to enter. Not that she needed permission.

After the superstorms, after the oceans rose and the government fractured and everything went to shit in a little under a year, the Network had risen out of nowhere. Some say they were inspired by the messages in Johnny Eternal's music. Jess's mother compared them to the hippies of her own mother's generation. Nobody much minded them, and their carnivals were always a good time.

Jess stops her walk in front of a man juggling a few unlit fire sticks. His skinny torso writhes with tattoos: tidal waves engulfing cities, a massive fire consuming an indistinct human form. "Who's that?"

He looks down at his stomach. "Nobody specific. It's just art."

She holds out her hand, though she doesn't quite know why. "I'm Jess."

He shakes back. "William."

"Aren't you afraid you'll burn yourself?" she asks, indicating the sticks. "When they're lit, I mean."

William starts juggling again. "I've been doing this for two years now. It's safe. I could teach you to do it."

Heat rises to Jess's face. "That's okay. I just want to watch."

He smiles and leads her to the edge of the gathering. He pulls a lighter from his jeans pocket and touches it to the tips of the sticks. "Suit yourself." With skilled, fluid motions, he juggles the flaming objects with ease, almost setting the trees around them ablaze.

He has control, Jess thinks. "So how long have you been traveling?"

William can't reply until he's finished the routine and the fire sticks are doused. "Three years. Almost since the beginning."

"You just . . . left everything behind?"

He squints. "What, you thinking about coming with?"

Jess shakes her head forcefully.

"Yeah, I wouldn't take you for the type. No offense. You either want to travel or you don't." William shrugs.

"I mean, I thought about it, yeah. But I'm really trying to get back to Pittsburgh. Or any Development Zone really. I'm not picky."

The tattooed man puts the fire sticks back in his marshmallow and takes a swig from a thermos. He doesn't offer Jess any of the mystery liquid. "I was an investment banker in Baltimore when the storm hit. Worked in a skyscraper overlooking the Chesapeake Bay, top floor. That's the only reason I survived. The entire city was destroyed, very few escaped."

Jess gets it. "You *had* to leave. You lost all your stuff."

An angry cast falls over his eyes, but he blinks it away. "It's not about *stuff*. You can't know what it was like, not if you didn't live through it. There were so many bodies laid out on the streets, just piled up like garbage. Mass graves. Even if I had an apartment to go back to, I couldn't." William pauses and takes another drink. "I died there too. A rescue bot breathed into me, woke me up. That's the only reason I'm still alive."

"I saw it on the news. Well, not you specifically."

"It changes you. We didn't rebuild the East Coast because we didn't want to. Nobody who lived through that ever wanted to go back *ever*. We're much happier this way."

Jess holds up her hands. "I'm not judging you."

"Some people do. Everyone here's been pretty nice though. It's only once you get closer to the Islands that they start getting a little squirrely."

Because you don't fit the aesthetic, Jess thinks. "So what time does the magic happen tomorrow?"

"Ten o'clock. I'll be doing some more of this," he says, pointing to the fire sticks. "Of course, you've already seen it for free."

Jess smiles. "I don't mind watching it again."

William smiles back but weakly. "Well, later."

Jess winds her way through the little tent village, searching for someone else to talk to, but everyone else seems busy in a way that they never are at the call center. For a moment, she feels a pang of jealousy. Surely there can be no New People here, doing this kind of work.

Unless they blend, she thinks, remembering Alicia in the bathroom. *Unless they remember.*

It's a choice between joining Dale in the game or going home, so she picks the latter. She'll be back here tomorrow morning, Saturday morning, maybe with Louisa too. Maybe the show will shock Louisa out of whatever funk she's gotten into.

And maybe I need it a little bit too, Jess thinks. Her steps feel just the slightest bit lighter.

11

THE MATS ARE LAID OUT, AND THE LIGHTS ON DALE'S BRICK OF A COMPUTER system are blinking, and four capsules of Trancium sit on a little tray on the chipped kitchen counter. Everything is just about ready.

Dale knocks on the door of his bedroom. Alicia had asked to rest up in there after he'd told her about tonight's plans. She opens it, not looking like someone who's taken a nap.

Voluntary low-power state, Dale thinks. *Not a nap.* "So you ready? Those guys should be here any minute."

"I'm not sure I can do this, Dale."

"It's not as scary as it seems. It can actually be a lot of fun. See, the—"

"I mean that I'm not sure that New People can plug in."

"Oh." Dale forgets sometimes that Alicia isn't quite a person.

"But I'll try it," she says, smiling. "I'll try it for you."

The buzzer rings, and Dale goes down to retrieve the middle-aged couple. They've brought their own mouthpieces, specially molded, very expensive compared to Dale's prefab ones. Theo plunks a bottle of wine on Dale's kitchen counter.

"Helps me to loosen up," he explains. Both of the men nod at Alicia. Either they don't know what she is—which is possible—or they just want to get on with the game.

Dale pours three glasses. "I hope it's not the gladiator scenario." He's played that one too many times, and now it's laced with bad memories that will never go away.

"We play whatever *they* want," Ray says.

It's true, Dale thinks. *We're just Islanders' pawns, used for these simulations because our reactions are more erratic and thus more interesting than a program would be. We have no say in this and never did.*

Dale passes around the tray of Trancium. Theo and Ray pop theirs immediately, but Alicia merely blinks at the colorful capsule. Dale mimes the act of swallowing.

"You place it in your mouth," he says, "and then just push it down." He gulps a mouthful of spit.

"I don't think I can do that."

Theo has already put his helmet on. It's his own equipment too, much nicer than Dale's pitted bike helmets. "Kid, we'd better get started."

Alicia frowns at the pill. "What should I do with this?"

"You swallow it," Dale says, trying his best to sound patient.

"I don't think I can do that," Alicia replies. But she makes a go at it anyway, popping the capsule into her mouth and rolling it around her cheeks a bit.

It's funny how she seems so human most of the time, Dale thinks, *until something like this comes up.* He wonders why Solfind didn't give the New People the ability to swallow food even if they didn't need to do it to live. It would help them blend in and give them a bit of pleasure besides.

Dale fits one of his own helmets over Alicia's head and shows her how to hold the wires between her teeth. When the three others are waiting for sleep on their mats, he doses himself, sets the program, and waits for his own translation to the gamespace.

A moment before he blacks out, Dale looks over at Alicia to see if she's comfortable. Her eyes are wide open.

Dale wakes in a city. A large city full of bustling crowds and fervent noise with more cars and billboards than he's seen even in Pittsburgh. The sun is high in the sky, and he tilts his face up, enjoying the heat. In front of him is an old cemetery, and in back of him is water.

That's the Atlantic Ocean, he thinks with a pang of terror.

He looks around for Alicia, Theo, and Ray. You never spawned too far from your fellow players. But then again, most scenarios weren't this busy.

Dale spots Ray's avatar next to a gyro stand and waves him over. "Hey, do you know where we are? I've never been in this one before."

"It does look familiar." Ray shakes his head, clearly lost in thought. "Can't quite put my finger on it."

Theo runs up. He's skinned in a businessman's suit and carries a briefcase. "Guys, we're in Boston."

One of the cities that went down, Dale thinks, *in the storm. The thing that kicked off the Break. Why would anyone want to watch a bunch of players reenact the fall of Boston?* "We need to find Alicia. This is her first game. She might be scared."

"Your other girlfriend," Theo snickers. Ray shoots his husband a playful look.

The three of them travel close together—easy to get separated in this crowd—and scan the passersby. "Alicia!" Dale yells. He startles when some of the crowd stare at him, at the three of them.

"Why can they see us?" Theo asks.

Dale and Ray both shrug, and the older man points at a picnic table on the green. "Let's go sit and wait for her. It'll be easier for her to find us if we stay in one place. And then we can try to figure out what this scenario is all about."

"Works for me," Dale says. The three of them take up spots at the table, and Theo slams the briefcase between them. He's the only one who spawned with gear.

Theo clicks open the briefcase. Inside are some folders and legal pads. Dale reaches for one, but Theo slaps his hand back.

"We have to do this right. I've never been in a scenario like this."

"Yeah, usually we just kill each other," Dale says. In every scenario he's been in, from the gladiator one to the Wild West Experience to wishful-thinking futuristic gamespaces, mass death had been the climax of the action. Islanders really liked watching that.

"I don't think we're supposed to do that this time." Theo hands one folder to Ray and another to Dale, then closes the briefcase.

Strategies for the Liquidation of Assets, Dale reads on the folder's cover, *presented by the Solfind Research and Development Team.* "Seems pretty dry."

"Oh, Jesus." Ray, who's already opened his folder, turns to show its contents to the other two. "Look at this shit."

It's a photograph of Boston—or what Dale assumes is Boston—after the storm. The skeletal structure of a giant, multi-story building lies like the corpse of a dead giant in the middle of a street. Dale thinks he can see bodies underneath it, though they could just be photographic artefacts.

He opens his own folder. It's much of the same except the structure he's looking at was clearly once a school. A crying child sits in the middle of a playground while an older man—a teacher?—lies broken in the forefront. His head has been torn off.

"What in the world?" Theo says, engrossed in what is surely his own pile of gore.

"Is this what it actually looked like?"

"Couldn't tell you," Ray says. "I remember some of this, but most of the reports weren't this bad. I mean, people died, but—"

"Look at this." Theo flips over his folder, and Dale sees that he in fact doesn't have a folder full of violent imagery but instead a memo.

In order to compartmentalize various consumer affinity groups, it might be advisable to . . . Dale looks at Theo. "Do you know what this says?"

"Son, I slung hash in the army for twenty years." Theo jabs his thumb at Ray. "But Ray here had a desk job."

Ray takes the folder and scans the neatly typed two-page document. "This can't be right. It says that Solfind caused the storm. That they have"—he squints at the fine print—"planted explosive devices throughout key areas of the Eastern Seaboard." The balding blond man shakes his head and tosses the folder back to Theo. "Conspiracy theories."

"I'm getting really worried about Alicia." Dale scans the crowd again and rubs his suddenly chilly arms. When they'd spawned, it had been a nice summer day, but now the wind is picking up. His digital skin prickles, all the fine little hairs standing on end.

"You two wait here," Theo says. "I'm gonna see if I can find the tripwire." He kisses Ray goodbye and saunters off in the direction of the old cemetery.

Every scenario comes built with a tripwire. If you need to bail for any reason, you can, though you usually won't get paid. In the gladiator scenario, it's located near the western gate where the lion pops out. Dale doesn't know where the tripwire could possibly be here. This scenario is so much bigger than any he's ever been in before.

Ray looks over more of the folders and scribbled-in pads. "Who would give us this stuff? This doesn't even feel like a game."

"Maybe it's some kind of mystery thing. Like we're supposed to figure out what's right or not." Dale looks cautiously at the churning Atlantic Ocean. "Or maybe the storm is coming."

"Can't be. That happened in the winter."

"Oh yeah." Somehow, Dale had forgotten.

Across the green, a mixed group of what look like college students throw around a Frisbee. Dale watches them for a time. One of the students' dogs is there with them, nipping at their heels, trying to catch the plastic disc.

One of the students suddenly shrieks, a high-pitched note that rattles Dale's head.

"Move, move!" Theo yells, barreling through the crowd, his foot overturning a picnic basket. "Everybody get out of the way!"

Dale turns to Ray, but he's already out on the green with his husband. Someone else has appeared there too.

Rachel, Dale thinks. He stuffs the folders back in the briefcase and carries it with him.

She's still dressed in the gladiator uniform, though it appears damaged. Her body is fuzzy, like something a bit too far away to see clearly, though the three of them are only a few feet away from her.

The Vaseline vision again, Dale thinks, remembering the original game with its tragic end.

Ray reaches out a hand and jerks it quickly back. "She's got defenses," he says, sucking on his fingertips.

Are we supposed to kill her? Dale wonders. This doesn't fit with the Boston scenario at all, not that he's gotten a great handle on what they're supposed to be doing in pre-Break Boston. "Rachel!"

"You know this person?"

Theo nods appreciatively.

"This boy does get around."

"She was part of my old group. The last time we played . . . it was bad. She had a seizure or something, and they all blamed me, and now she's here." Dale sticks his own arm out, but his chest lurches as an electric shock runs through his body, similar to the ones every player gets when exiting gamespace. "And Alicia isn't."

"Maybe she's the tripwire," Ray says, though he's clearly just throwing out ideas. "Hang on. I'll go see if I can find something non-conductive."

"Rachel, can you hear us?" Dale shouts, though he's not sure why. She's right here.

The fuzzy woman focuses her gaze on them, both Dale and Theo. Then she lunges, crashing into whatever invisible barrier separates them, falling on her face.

"Here," Ray says. He's holding a plank of wood.

"What do we do, just poke her?" Dale tries it anyway, and the plank slides off an invisible barrier five inches from her avatar.

Theo leads him away. "Now, kid, we're going to be waking up soon. I don't know where your *other* girlfriend is, but unless we're all together, we could lose her in this."

"I can't lose another one." Tears spring to Dale's eyes. "And this time, it *would* be my fault. Because I couldn't find her."

Ray's watching the Rachel-containing invisible bubble intently. The gladiator woman inside is saying something, but no sound is coming out. *He's trying to read her lips,* Dale realizes.

"I feel it coming," Theo says. "Do you feel it?"

"Yeah," Dale replies as the sensation of the scenario slipping away from him becomes apparent. His stomach lurches, and his vision begins to get blurry. "It's starting."

The two of them collect Ray and wait for their transport back, staking a space only a few feet away from Rachel.

"I'm sorry," Dale says with exaggerated lip movements in case she can read lips too. He brushes the back of his hand across his eyes and takes one more look at the terrifying specter of the Atlantic Ocean.

The three of them wake up simultaneously. Ray pulls himself upright, his breath sucking in with pain. "Where's the girl?"

Dale manages to move his paralyzed eyes far enough to the right to glimpse Alicia's mat, but she's not on it. His heart pounds. It was one thing to leave your mind behind but your body? "Alicia!" he manages to yell, fighting the temporary sickness. The Johnny Eternal record—a mid-career jazz fusion experiment that hadn't quite worked out called *Hyperbaric Lantern*—sings its last few notes and ceases its spinning.

His bedroom door opens. The New Woman walks out, her skirt suit as freshly pressed as if she'd just ironed the thing. Dale absently wonders what the hell it's made out of. "Hello, Dale. Hello, Ray and Theo."

Theo takes his mouthpiece out and blinks several times. "She was never in. They *can't* go under."

"Alicia, what happened?" Dale can already tell he's going to have to drag the story out of her.

Alicia sits on the couch, her hands nervously moving to the hemline of her skirt. She twists it as she speaks. "The pill never took." She points at a barely digested capsule on Dale's shitty indoor-outdoor rug. "I tried putting myself into a low-power state when I was plugged in, but it was . . . bad."

"You had a nightmare," Dale says.

Theo wrings the numbness from his hands. "Were you in Boston?"

Alicia gasps. "How did you know?"

"We were there too."

The New Woman blinks a few times and then stands and heads for the door. Dale stares at her, not yet able to stand himself. Powerless to stop her from leaving. "Where are you going?"

"Back to Pittsburgh. Thank you for your hospitality, Dale Carter."

"No, wait!" Dale curses under his breath at the effects of the return from gamespace that keep him from running after her. "What's wrong?"

"That wasn't a nightmare," Alicia says. "Those are my memories, and all of you were inside them. I have to go be rewritten by Solfind." She looks at Dale, her eyes thick silver pools. "I'd say I'll never forget you, but that would be a lie."

Dale feels a jolt of electricity through his upper arm as he uses the couch to brace himself. "You're not leaving until we all figure out what happened. My friend was in there too. Did you see her? Rachel?"

"Maybe we *should* let her go," Ray says with a spooked expression.

Theo raises his voice. "Nobody's going anywhere. Now I've played a *lot* of games in the last three years, and I've never seen anything like this." He stares the New Woman down. "You know more than you're letting on, missy."

She slowly moves back to the couch, sits down again. "It's a long story."

"It's Saturday," Dale says. "And my day is wide open."

12

Come on, Lou," Jess says, turning the volume of her sister's music down. "Get ready. We're going out." She's a little surprised that Louisa is up so early on a Saturday morning, but she remembers the sounds and music that drift down every night from Louisa's cramped room. Louisa hasn't been sleeping.

"Turn that back on," Louisa says. "That's Johnny's best album, *Busted Synapse.*"

"I know what it is." She prods at Louisa until her little sister drags herself out of bed.

Louisa yawns. "Is Mom back?"

"Yeah, she was home when I got back yesterday." Not that they'd really interacted. Her mom was camped out like usual on her chair in the living room, locked into the feed. She hadn't told Jess where she'd been. "The Network is in town."

"That's cool."

Jess spins her sister to face her. "Now I know you're sad about something, and you don't have to tell me what it is, but we're going to see their show in an hour and that's final."

"I have homework."

Yeah, like you do your homework, Jess thinks. "Then you'd better get started now."

Louisa sullenly sits down at her desk and pulls a workbook out of her backpack. It's covered with doodles, much like Jess's sketch pad at work. *She'll graduate, so she can get a job where she can be paid to do the exact same thing,* Jess realizes. *Circle of life.*

There's a knock at the door, and after giving her mom a minute to answer it, Jess goes down to see who it is. It's a short, plump woman with a slightly familiar face. "Wait, you're—"

"Rachel," the woman says. "I'm in your friend Dale's gaming group. Used to be anyway." She peers behind Jess to where her mom is lounging like a slug with her feed reader glued to her face. Every so often, she lifts a cheese curl to her mouth. "Is this a bad time?"

"Uh, come in." Jess leads Rachel down to her basement room. "Lou, you'd better be working up there!"

Rachel sits down on Jess's bed, and Jess takes the floor. The balding carpet that covers the concrete does nothing to cushion Jess's ass. Jess mentally goes over the story Dale told her about how Rachel had been "lost" in the game, and that's why Terry had punched out his front teeth. She feels slightly angry at Rachel, even though it's not her fault. Before she can begin to figure out what to say, Rachel speaks up, her voice spilling out in one giant mess.

"When I was in the game last time, I kind of broke away from the others, got lost in my own world. Not on purpose, it just happened. Nothing in there should be able to hurt you. But I guess it did? When I woke up, they told me that Dale hurt me, but that can't be true. Can it? I know you're his friend. You can find this out for me." She looks expectantly at Jess.

"I don't play," Jess says, trying to hold off another of Rachel's fast-paced speeches. "But I know he wouldn't hurt you on purpose. He's a good guy."

"Can you tell him I'm here, that I'm okay? I really am okay. They took me to the clinic, but by the time I got there, I was all better. Which was good because then we didn't have to pay."

Rachel moves her hands around a lot when she talks. Jess wants to push them back down in her lap.

"But also—and this is *really* weird, so I haven't been in the game since then? I kind of don't want to ever go back except I need the money. But I was at the mini-mart—that's where I work, at least for now—just hanging out behind the counter, and I . . . went back."

"To the game?"

Rachel takes a deep breath. "Yeah, it must have been. I mean, it wasn't *here*."

"What did it look like?" Jess blurts.

"I was still in that same stupid gladiator costume, and I was in a city. Not a

Development Zone but like a real city, like before the Break. It could have been New York."

Or Boston, Jess thinks, remembering Alicia's words. "And what happened?"

"Well, Dale was there. And these two older guys, one of them was black. They kept trying to talk to me and pull me in, but I was . . . stuck." Rachel mimes for a bit. "Then it ended, and I was all passed out on the floor. Got a pretty bad bruise on my butt. I sure hope I don't get fired. I need that job."

"That's Dale's new group," Jess says. "Was there anyone else there? A woman?"

"Nope, but I know you need four to get in, so . . ." Rachel makes an indistinct motion with her hands. "They must have been *somewhere.*"

Jess takes out her phone. "Let's call him. I'm sure he'll want to know you're okay. He's been talking about you nonstop for three days now." *And he took several punches for you,* Jess thinks, though she figures she shouldn't upset Rachel even more.

"Terry would kill me if he knew I'm here. He gets so irrational. Once he gets an idea in his head, then that's it, that's the truth. Can't be reasoned with. He's such a creeper."

"I believe you." Jess dials Dale's number, but it goes straight to voicemail. "You don't feel weird at all?"

"A couple more nightmares, but that's usual after a bad gaming session." Rachel shakes her head. "And that last run with Dale was a *bad* session. So bad."

Jess sends Dale a text—making sure to mark it *urgent, hurry*—and turns back to Rachel. "I'm not sure what I can do for you, but I'll make sure to let Dale know you're okay."

"Thanks," Rachel says, getting unsteadily to her feet. "I don't blame him. Like really I don't. It's just one of those glitches. But anyway, thanks again. I'll show myself out."

Well, that'll take a load off Dale's mind, Jess thinks. But how could Rachel have seen his game? Jess doesn't know much about gaming, but she knows enough to know that this isn't the way it's supposed to work. Each scenario is a world unto itself: there is no overlap. *Very strange.*

She goes up to Louisa's room, not surprised to see that her sister is back on the bed, the music cranked way up. A different album from the sound of it. This one features a horn section. "Come on, Lou. It's time to leave."

—∿—

By the time they've gotten to the park, the carnival is in full swing. A woman with a face full of piercings holds out a basket for suggested donations, and even though she can't really afford it, Jess drops in two skins.

Louisa stares at a contortionist, folding himself into an orange crate. Jess pulls her sister along.

"I was watching that."

"But the fire dancing is about to start," Jess says, thinking of William. "It's really good."

Louisa tilts her head. "Is that Johnny Eternal?"

Jess realizes that it is, though a different album than they had played on her previous visit to the campsite. *How many albums does that guy have anyway?* "Come on. I'll buy you a pop."

Her little sister tears herself away from the contortionist and follows Jess past the other exhibits to the stage at the edge of the park. The show's already started, and Jess catches a glimpse of William. He doesn't seem to notice her.

The music swells, and thankfully, it isn't more Johnny Eternal. A woman with electric-green hair pinned in a bun at the top of her head sets two hula hoops aflame and begins to spin them on her forearms.

Louisa gasps. "Is she going to die?"

"No, they know what they're doing." The woman stumbles, and one of the hoops lands on the ground near the audience. A crew member douses it with a pre-filled bucket of water. "I think."

William's routine is next, and his clubs are already lit. He tosses the three of them around for a little while and slowly incorporates two more, thrown to him by others standing in the wings. The girl with the hoops looks impressed.

An older woman digs clawlike fingers into Jess's side and slips a note into her palm. "Here, take this."

Annoyed, Jess jams the leaflet into her pocket. "I'm here to watch my friend," she mutters. But the anonymous messenger is already gone.

Louisa gazes at William, transfixed. "Do you think I can grow up to do this?"

"No, Lou. You want to grow up to be better than this."

Later, after six different performers have all done their routines, Jess winds her way to the front. "I made it!" she says to William.

He nods at her, blank-faced. "Thanks for coming."

"I told you I'd be back." She waits for his reply, but he just continues cleaning up. *He doesn't remember me,* she thinks. *Well, this was a waste.*

"Let's go see more things," Louisa says, finally into the event.

Jess suddenly wishes she were anywhere but here. Still, she lets her sister lead her to another clearing where a play is being performed. It's something about the storm and the Break that followed, and Jess is instantly bored.

She retrieves the pamphlet from her purse. *Join us on the traveling circuit,* it reads, *for a brighter future.* Inside, glossy pictures show various bands of Network members on their stops around the country.

They're recruiting, she thinks. *Well, let them.* Jess knows where her future is, and it's not with these people, some of whom can't even figure out when a person is actively flirting with them. She starts to wad the pamphlet up but decides to keep it for Louisa, who's happier than she's been in a year.

Out in the clearing, a woman sets herself adrift on a papier-mâché rowboat, searching for the "heart of the Atlantic." The smell of fried food wafts over the heads of the two dozen or so audience members as a passing vendor hawks her wares.

Louisa squeezes Jess's hand. "This is the best part."

"How would you know?" Jess replies, not unkindly. "You haven't seen it before."

"I just know," she says, sighing contentedly.

13

ALICIA, DALE, RAY, AND THEO SIT IN A CIRCLE, CROSS-LEGGED ON THE mats. The three humans' gamespace sickness is almost gone. Each holds a steaming cup of coffee except for Alicia. She fidgets a little, something Dale hasn't seen her do before.

"I *have* to leave," she says. "I could have hurt you."

"How?" Ray says, taking a sip of coffee. "Nothing in there is real."

She looks Dale in the eyes. "Your friend Rachel was hurt."

Dale reaches over and touches her wrist. She's colder than he thought she would be, her skin completely smooth and hairless. He instinctively jerks his hand back. "Did you see her in there? Is she okay?"

"I see a lot of things in my head, Dale. Even more of them lately." She closes her eyes and shudders.

"Those reports," Theo says, "and those pictures. They said that Solfind caused the storm. Care to explain that one?"

Alicia draws her knees up under her chin. "None of *their* employees died in the storm. They were evacuated to the auxiliary offices in Nebraska. And Solfind was researching weather machines before then. That's all I know."

"It isn't enough," Ray says.

"I know it, okay? I can feel it." She rubs her arms. "The storm wasn't natural. Why did it hit the cities only and with such precision?"

Dale remembers feed preachers claiming the storm was a punishment for the cities' sins of greed and fornication. Few people took them seriously, even here in West Virginia. "Where did you get the pictures?"

"I took them," she says, "with my eyes."

They all sit in silence for a little while, and Dale refills their coffee cups. Dale is torn between wishing that Theo and Ray would go home and not wanting them to leave. For some reason, he's afraid to be alone with Alicia. *But that's stupid,* he thinks. *Why would I ever be afraid of her?*

"That *is* weird," Ray says. "The plans for the Development Zones were drawn up within about a month after the storm. Twenty million people died, but society went on."

"I guess I never thought of it that way," Dale says. "We didn't exactly just 'go on.'" *At least not here,* he thinks.

Theo pipes up. "I just figured Solfind had a lot of eggheads on board. Didn't they used to be a computer company?"

"They're an everything company," Dale says. Even the Trancium that players used to access the gamespace came from a Solfind lab, originally developed as a treatment for narcolepsy. "Alicia, do you think Trancium plays into this at all?"

She shrugs. "Anything's possible."

Ray stands and stretches. "I think we'd better get home. I could sleep for weeks after that game. Did they even pay us?"

"I don't know why they would," Dale says, "seeing as how we just got shunted into Alicia's head." He checks his account anyway for shits and giggles. "Oh, holy fuck."

"What is it?" Theo says, his helmet already tucked beneath his arm.

Dale angles the screen toward them. "There's five thousand skins in here."

After Ray and Theo have left—Theo openly regretting their promise to let Dale have the entire share—Dale rolls up the mats and puts away the wires, mouthpieces, and helmets. With shaking hands, he makes himself a sandwich. *One measly slice of baloney on moldy white bread,* he thinks, *but not for long.*

Alicia's still perched on the couch, watching Dale intently. "Maybe it's a mistake."

"Doesn't matter if it is. I transferred it. It's in my account."

"What are you going to do with it?"

Dale hasn't gotten that far. "Well, the rent for one. And I can fix up my teeth. Take Jess someplace nice." He lights a cigarette. Pretty soon, he won't even have to ration these.

"It's not *that* much money, Dale."

Dale takes a bite of his tasteless sandwich, the food stinging the exposed roots of his tooth nubs. "It's a fucking lot of money to me."

Alicia just wraps her hands around her shoulders as if she's cold, even though she can't possibly be. *It's summer, and she's not alive,* Dale thinks.

The doorbell rings. Dale peeks past the chain and breathes a sigh of relief when he sees it's just Jess. He flings the door open wide. "I've got great news."

Jess's line of vision grazes over Alicia. "So do I. Your friend Rachel is alive."

Dale hasn't even thought about Rachel since seeing the windfall, and he feels a little stab of shame. "D-Did you see her?"

Jess leans over and plucks his sandwich off the counter, takes a bite. "She came to my house."

"She did? Is she okay?"

"Got some diarrhea of the mouth, but yeah, she's fine. She said she saw you though. She wanted you to know that. I tried to call and tell you, but you didn't pick up your damn phone."

Dale's forehead wrinkles. "I saw her too, but it wasn't *her.* I saw her in the game. But that's just code."

"Well, this code saw you and told me all about it. She said you were in some city, you and those two guys from BurgerMat . . ."

"We were in Boston," Alicia says from the couch. "It's where I'm from. Where I was first *used* anyway."

Jess ignores her. "As I was saying, she's fine except for the chatter-mouth."

"She's always been like that."

"What's *your* news?"

Dale starts to tell her about the money. He's five seconds away from doing it. But something in him holds it back. "It's nothing."

"It's not *nothing.* Spit it out."

He looks at Alicia who seems to catch his drift. "Oh, I just got some new Johnny Eternal bootlegs from someone on the feed. His live show from last year."

"Thrilling," she says, dropping next to Alicia on the couch.

Alicia stands up. "Doesn't anyone want to talk about the game? Or about what I saw in Boston? What I *know* is going on?"

Jess looks at Alicia and back at Dale. "Did she tell you those conspiracy theories too?"

He shrugs. "There could be some truth to them."

"But it doesn't *matter*." Jess crosses her legs underneath her. "Solfind ruined the country, so what? We still have to live here. Nothing is going to change. Do you think they're just going to round up the executives in a little police car and ferry them off to jail?" She laughs over-exuberantly. "And then we'll be heroes, and the ocean goes back to where it used to be, and New York and Boston spring back up like they were hiding there all the time."

Alicia stamps her foot, making the floorboards shake. "The truth *does* matter!"

"Who's going to leak this, 'Alicia'?" Jess draws air quotes. "You New People? They'll just shut you off and make more of you. Us? Please. It's Solfind's world. We're just living in it. And you're not even alive."

"That's *enough*, Jess." Dale slides into the office chair in his living room. It's slightly musty; he'd pulled it from a trash pile not too long ago. "I think we need to go back into Alicia's head. Maybe we can get more clues, more direction about how we should proceed." *And more money*, he thinks.

"Hell no," Jess says.

"No," Alicia replies. "I won't harm you. Or Theo and Ray."

He glares at her. "I thought you wanted to take down the company or whatever. That's why you ran away, right?"

"Not exactly," Alicia says in a small voice.

"She said she wanted to keep her memories," Jess says. "Which is the stuff you just saw, I guess."

Alicia wrings her hands, flustered.

Dale is concerned that her electrical powers will discharge suddenly, take down this entire apartment complex.

"I don't know what I want, okay? I don't know what's right."

"What's right is letting me, Ray, and Theo back into your head, so we can run another game."

"But I'll have a nightmare!" *She sounds like a child,* Dale thinks, *afraid of monsters under the bed.*

"Nightmares can't hurt you. Or well, they don't hurt *us*. And maybe we should get Rachel in on this too if she'll risk it again."

Jess bites her fingernails. "She said Terry would kill her if she tries to meet up with you."

"Then I'll have to meet her in secret. I feel like she's a key in all of this. Or at least a part." He drops to his knees in front of Alicia. "Please say you'll let us back in. If you care about the truth, you'll do this."

Alicia bites her lip, the computational unit in her head clearly in overdrive. Finally, she relents. "Okay, I'll do it. For the truth and for you, Dale Carter." She looks at Jess. "Are you going to come in too, Jessica?"

"Trancium makes me sick," Jess says. She doesn't add the other part, the fact that it doesn't work on her. But Dale remembers.

"We'll do it Monday night. That'll give me enough time to find Rachel, get Theo and Ray roped back in, and maybe find some other players." Dale thinks Sara will be into it if he decides to show her the last game's take.

"I need to go," Jess says, standing up.

"Will you be back on Monday? For the game?"

Jess frowns at him. "You don't need me for that."

But I do, Dale thinks.

14

On Monday morning, Jess walks the mile-and-change to the call center. A sun-shower pelts her face with light, warm mist, and she wipes at her eyes with the back of her hand. She's late for work, but she doesn't care. She swerves onto a gravel path that connects to the park, which is almost but not quite on the way.

The Network is packing up. The collapsible mushroom-shaped tents lie in puckered piles of nylon on the ground, and the smell of diesel hangs in the air, the warming engines growling at the park's edge.

Jess scans the crowd, finds William. Even though it means she'll definitely be late, she goes up to him anyway.

"I came to your show."

"Oh yeah? Did you like it?" His tent is already collapsed and bagged and placed next to his show props.

"I wish I could do something like this. Just run away from my troubles."

William smiles. "Well, you *could*."

Jess looks out at the other members of the traveling troupe who are loading their own collapsed homes and suitcases into a long line of cars and trucks adjoining the park. One of them, a large, boxy van that seems slightly less decrepit than the others, crackles with vibrant swirls of primary colors, so bright they almost give Jess a headache. "No, I can't. I have loans."

"That's too bad. Hey, I'll catch you later, okay? We'll be coming through again in, uh, about eight months."

She looks back at him, at his rippling tattoos. "It'll be winter."

"Space heaters," he says as he flings his tent on his back and takes a bag into each hand.

The silence hangs for a moment between them, though Jess thinks it might only be noticeable to her. "I have to go to work. So see ya, I guess." Jess feels mournful, though she doesn't quite know why.

"The loan companies can't make you pay them back if you're with us, you know," he says like an afterthought. "We count as a religious group for the purposes of the federal government."

Well, you kind of are one, she thinks, remembering the pamphlet. "Be safe. Send me a postcard sometime."

William gets a distant look in his eyes. "We don't really do that."

"Oh," Jess says, embarrassed.

So that's it then. Back to work she goes. Jess doesn't know if he was leading her on this whole time or if he just didn't realize she was flirting. *But what's he gonna do?* she thinks. *Stop traveling and stay in Wheeling with me? He's happy on the road. And probably not even interested.* Jess pulls her hood tight over her head. The rain is picking up.

The moment she steps into the call center, something feels off. Jess spots Kathy and waves at her. "This place looks deader than usual."

The supervisor sighs. "We had to make more cuts."

"But you just *did* that!"

"It's not enough. Look, Nowicki, we're probably not going to last out the month. Enjoy this while it lasts."

Enjoy isn't quite the word Jess would use. "Is this because of Alicia?"

"No, this comes from headquarters. She'll be out too."

"Does she—I mean, it—know?"

Kathy's eyes track to Alicia, who is already at its desk. "Ask her yourself. I have to pack up my office."

Jess walks over to Alicia. She forces herself to place a hand on the New Woman's shoulder. The woman-thing makes a shuddering sound, which Jess could almost take for crying if she didn't know better. "Heya."

Alicia looks up at her. "I have to go back."

Jess plops into her own chair, spins around once. "Dale will take care of you."

"I *want* to go back," the New Woman says. "I need to be rewritten. The nightmares . . . they haven't stopped. They're happening even during the day, even when I'm not in a low-power state." She shudders. "They're happening right now."

Out of the corner of her eye, Jess catches a glimpse of Kathy sneaking out of the office early, a box full of office supplies balanced on one arm. Jess picks up her sketchbook. "You owe it to Dale to run one last game. You promised him."

"I know," the New Woman says. It lets out another one of those strange cries. "I'll go back tomorrow morning after the game. Before they all wake up."

Jess sketches out the framework of a building that might be the call center. "What are they going to find in your head, Alicia?"

The New Woman stares straight ahead. Jess would give almost anything for a call to come in right then, break the silence. Jess wonders if the woman-thing is having a flashback right now. She draws another few lines on her sketch pad and counts down the seconds until lunch.

They're closing us down, she types to Dale on the phone held underneath her plywood desk. She doesn't send it. She's not sure why.

When lunch is over and Kathy still hasn't come back, Jess leaves too. *Fuck it,* she thinks. *If they don't care, neither do I. And I never did care about this job, not one little bit.* It's time for her to finally take charge of her own life.

She turns around one last time. Alicia is at the lunchroom window, pawing at it like a kitten in a shelter. The rain's still falling, and Jess's shoes squeak like pistons all the way home.

The house is silent when Jess returns.

"Lou?" she yells. "Mom?" Flicking on all the lights reveals an empty house. Her mom's recliner with attached feed reader sits vacant. A note on its seat reads "Bingo."

Jess pulls open the refrigerator door. Nothing but a loaf of bread and half a jar of olives. She takes out both and makes herself a snack.

I need to look at my options, Jess thinks. It's impossible for her to stay in Wheeling any longer: there are no jobs, there are no contacts, and if she has to stay one more night in that basement with the squawk of her mother's feed drifting down, she'll scream.

Instead of creating New People, why couldn't they have improved us? There'd been a few small movements in that direction before the series of superstorms and the Break that followed, treatments designed to remove the need for sleep and improve general health. That's all stopped though.

Jess thinks back to a couple she'd been friends with in college, David and Katia, who'd both emigrated to Belize after graduation. There were certain pockets of the world Solfind hadn't touched, and anyone who could pony up around twenty thousand skins could buy themselves a few more years away from conglomerates. She'd considered it when her lease in the Pittsburgh Development Zone had run out, but where would she get the money?

They'll get everyone in the end anyway, she thinks. *There's no place on earth where Solfind can't reach, given time.*

The light in the kitchen has turned gray. It's almost sunset. Jess washes and dries the dish slowly. Her arms feel dead and heavy.

"She should have been home by now," Jess mutters, thinking of her mom. "Both of them should be." She wonders if Louisa had even left the house that morning and slowly ascends the stairs just in case.

She can't be home, Jess tells herself. *She'd have one of those damn records playing.* She knocks on the door, which swings open, not even latched. She slips inside.

Inside to where Louisa lays with an empty pill bottle in one hand and a note in the other. The stilled record sits on the turntable.

"Lou!" Jess screams. Whatever drugs—Trancium?—she'd swallowed are fully active, and her sister's eyes flutter in the deepest part of a blissed-out sleep. She snatches the note from Louisa's hand.

It's the lyrics page from a Johnny Eternal record, some of the lines highlighted with Magic Marker. *Come and meet me in a better world,* she reads. *We have everything for boys and girls.*

"Fucking dreck." Jess slaps her little sister across the face a few times. "Wake up, Lou!"

You've seen Dale on this stuff, Jess reminds herself, *and you even took it once. Louisa isn't going to die.*

Jess just has to wait for Louisa to come around. She puts the record back on, hoping that her sister's love of the immensely, inexplicably popular folksinger will bring her back to consciousness.

It doesn't. As Johnny whines away, plinking out chords on his poorly tuned guitar, Louisa seems to get even deeper into the zone. Her arms and legs begin to twitch in a rhythmic pattern.

"Lou?" She shakes her sister's foot. "C'mon. Get up."

Nothing. Louisa's body continues to jerk, but she doesn't get up, and she doesn't speak.

We can't afford a doctor, Jess thinks, *not unless both of us want to be in hock for the rest of our lives.* As she continues to try to rouse Louisa, Jess feels both of their futures slip away. "Wake up, Lou. Please wake up."

Her sister mouths words, and though Jess can't read her lips, she's obviously acting out some kind of dream. Just like Dale does when he takes Trancium in the game or just for fun. He spins the same records Louisa does.

Well, of course. Johnny Eternal's the most popular musician in the country, though God knows why. She picks up the cover of the album that's spinning. *Relapse and Reveal.* The photograph is of a lifeless desert, neither Johnny nor the title nor anything else printed on it.

But in the background, near a group of saguaros, is a sort of glimmer. A shimmer? It hurts Jess's head to look at it too long, and she sets the album down.

Jess makes a decision. She picks Louisa off the bed—she weighs nothing at all—and carries her downstairs, sets her on the couch.

She packs everything the both of them will need, limiting herself to two suitcases of clothes, toiletries, and a few books. She pointedly leaves behind the Johnny Eternal albums and record player.

Jess phones a cab. The cost is exorbitant, but she can afford it, just barely. Pittsburgh Development Zone, one-way trip. She'll figure everything out when they get there. Louisa will be awake by then.

"I won't let you stay here," she says to her sister. "This place is a trap. And it's only going to get worse."

Louisa's eyes pop open. She looks around at where she is, neck and hands moving slowly and with obvious pain. Jess recognizes it as the post-Trancium sickness. Her little sister's glassy eyes focus on Jess. Louisa cries.

"Where are we going, Jess?" Her voice is shaky and thin. "Why do we have suitcases?"

"Shush. I'm taking you to the city."

Louisa stands but immediately grips the arm of the couch for stability. She's still too weak to walk. "I don't want to go."

"Lou, I'm not going to sit around and watch you abuse drugs while listening to those stupid records. That's no kind of life. And if Mom isn't going to help you, then *I will*."

Louisa wipes a trembling hand over her wet face. "You don't get it, Jess. I was happy there. We're all happier there. It's the better world."

A car horn beeps, and lights flash. It's now fully dark out. Jess walks Louisa to the door, and her sister is in no position to refuse. The cab is automated, so she just scans her phone across the window.

Louisa's still crying in the backseat but at least not saying anything.

"Drive," Jess says, and the automated chauffeur complies, speeding them toward the Pittsburgh Development Zone. Toward Jess and Louisa's future, whatever it may be.

15

IN THE END, DALE MANAGED TO ROPE FIVE PEOPLE BESIDES HIMSELF INTO THE game: Ray and Theo, Sara, Rachel, and Caden, his old gaming partner who hadn't really blamed him for what happened. And that wasn't counting Alicia who didn't count.

Because she is the game, Dale thinks. He'd asked her to stay in a low-power state until everyone got to the apartment, but that was less to reserve her power—New People don't work that way—than to lower the chances of her backing out.

He pours the customary snacks—stale Chex mix swiped from the dumpster of the mini-mart—into bowls and waits for the others to show up. He's still hoping that Jess will make an appearance but knows it's not very likely.

Stubborn as fuck, he thinks. *That's my Jess.*

The buzzer sounds, and he throws open the door to find Sara, his old manager at BurgerMat.

"I thought you said you were going to be late. Because of the shifts."

"Yeah well, no shifts anymore. They're shutting us down. BurgerMat won the right to fully automate. They don't need us no more." She runs her hand across Dale's top-of-the-line, pre-Break stereo system, the one object he'd never part with. "Couple of suits came in this afternoon, said we weren't making any money, and made me leave immediately. Got to keep a pretty nice doggie bag though."

Jess was right, he thinks without surprise. *There is no future here.* "Were they New People?"

"What do *you* think?" Sara catches sight of Alicia, lounging on Dale's bed in the next room. "I hate them. And now you want us to go *into* one of them. For what?"

Dale shakes his head. "It's not like that. Alicia's no fan of Solfind herself. She ran away from them."

"You said there'd be a big payday at the end of this, Carter. You'd better not be lying."

"There is." If the mysterious benefactor who'd given him five thousand skins doesn't make another reappearance now, he'll split the original windfall between all of them equally. Even after the split, he'll have enough to fix his teeth. At least, he hopes.

Sara eats a bit of the stale Chex mix. "What are you spinning?"

"*Shockwave Fantastic, Down on Thirty, An Interruption.*" He thumps the side of the stereo system. "Classic era."

"Nice," she says and takes a swig of tap water. He never had gotten around to stocking any beer.

The buzzer chimes again, and it's Ray and Theo, once again carting their own equipment. The two men nod at Sara. Dale starts to roll out the mats.

"So let me get this straight," Theo says, his hands gesturing. "We're going into the head of your main girlfriend, plus this other girlfriend you're cheating on her with, but not that angry girlfriend who was here the other day."

"None of these women are my girlfriend, Theo. They're just women." *Or at least woman-like,* he thinks.

Theo's face cracks into a grin. "I'm just messing with you."

Dale looks out the window. Rachel and Caden aren't late—the game isn't scheduled to start until seven—but he finds himself worried about Terry. He'd finally just worked up the nerve to call Rachel at the mini-mart she worked at a few hours a week.

They'll shut that one down too, he thinks. *And Jess's call center can't be far behind.*

Alicia enters the room, woken from her low-power state. Sara jerks her head away, toward a banal conversation with Ray. "I'm ready," the New Woman says.

"We're waiting on two more." He fetches his bottle of Trancium from its hidey-hole. There're only a dozen pills left. But that's more than enough for this final ride.

Stomps coming down the hallway make the snacks in the bowl jump.

"Someone's out there," Theo says, and Dale looks through the peephole, hoping to see Rachel and Caden. Instead, it's a muscle-bound white guy with a bad sunburn and a newly shaved head. Terry.

"Oh shit," Dale says. "Everyone, stay calm."

They all blink at him.

"Right, you don't know him. Anyway, that's the guy that broke my face. He's an asshole. And he blames me for hurting a friend of ours even though she's fine. She was supposed to be here tonight. I think he found out about it."

Sara gets a wry expression on her face. "You have the most interesting friends, Dale."

"So don't *panic* or anything," he says, "just be alert." A few pounds land on the door in quick succession, shaking it at the hinges. "I guess you can panic a little."

Alicia perks her head up and strides toward the door. She motions for everyone else to stay back. She flings the door open and throws herself on Terry. A whiff of ozone hits the air.

The lunk smirks at them and pulls a device the size of a box of matches from his pocket. A grill on the side exhales what looks like gas.

"He's blocking my signal," Alicia says. "I can't shock him." She still seems to be stronger than him though and shoves him to the ground, pinning him. There's a terrifying crack. It takes a moment for Dale to realize that Alicia has broken one of Terry's arms. Terry howls, though not as loudly as Dale would have expected.

"What do you *want* from me, Terry?" Dale says. "You know Rachel is fine. You've known that from the beginning. So what the fuck's your problem?"

He grins even from his pinned position, Alicia holding him down. "I want those five thousand skins. And your robot."

Dale's eyes flick to Alicia. "She's a person."

Terry takes another gulp of air. "Not to Solfind."

"She's a person to me. To all of us." He looks back into the apartment; Sara is rolling her eyes. "Wait, how do you know about the money?"

"You really need to get a better password, Carter."

Alicia looks up at him. "I can hold him as long as you want." *She could kill him,* Dale thinks, *but she won't.*

"Let him up. Let him go." She does, and Terry rises to his feet, coughing.

"Guess I'm calling the company then." He takes out his phone with his good hand. Dale wonders if he preemptively took something to block the pain just in case the woman-thing beat him up again. He seems too functional for that not to be the case. "I'm gonna get a reward for that runaway rescue bot. A *big* one."

Dale looks at Alicia, but she isn't doing anything, just gazing at Terry with an expression of resignation. "You're not going to *stop* him?"

"It's time, Dale. We need to start the game. You can explore a great deal of my mind before they take me away."

"But Caden and Rachel—"

She shuts the door behind her; Terry is still gloating. "We cannot wait. Please, tell them to start." She catches the eye of each of them in turn. "Start!"

Dale sighs. "Helmets on, guys." Dale drops the needle to the record and turns the volume way, way up. He passes around the blue-and-yellow pills. "Let's do this."

—⋀⋀⋀—

"I don't think we're in Boston this time," Theo says.

Dale materializes next to him, the two of them on a featureless plain that extends out to the limits of Dale's sight. He squints, looking for the others, but there's no trace of them. "What do we do?"

"We walk."

There's no gear at Dale's side, no gun or broadsword. His simulated outfit is the same as his one in reality: stained T-shirt, rumpled jeans. "Maybe it didn't work."

"Shush." Theo stops him short with an arm. "I hear something."

A groan like a dying motor picks up to Dale's left. He and Theo both turn to the sound. "I guess we go that way," Dale says.

"So who *did* put that money into your account?"

"It can't be anyone good." Dale shrugs. "Could have been a mistake."

"Then why do you think going back in will give us more of it?"

"Man, I don't know." Dale picks up his pace. He doesn't know how long he's been out in the real world. For all he knows, the cops could already be at his apartment about to wake up all of them and cart them down to the criminal justice division of the Northern West Virginia Undeveloped Zone. "But maybe it will help Alicia. Or we can find out more stuff about Solfind."

Theo hustles to keep up with Dale. "They're in the army now too. That's why I had to leave. They forced me out."

"That's good, right? Then it's not real people dying."

"You don't think Alicia is real?"

Dale glares at him. "Of course, she's real. I mean, they exist. They think and all. It's just different."

Theo snorts. "If you say so."

"What I mean is . . ." But Dale isn't sure what he means. In the right light and in the right headspace, Alicia is as human as he is. She's a *better* version of him. Dale doesn't want to be a bigot like Jess. But he can't pretend that Alicia and Jess are the same. "Well, they're programmed for the work they do, so they're not as afraid of dying."

"I think everyone's afraid of dying. Doesn't matter if it's a soldier or a bug, nobody wants to die."

Dale pictures Alicia running away to keep from being rewritten, attempting to hold onto her personality. Maybe rewriting is a form of death to New People? And she'd certainly been afraid of that, enough to try her luck in an Undeveloped Zone and camp out under the stars. "You're right, Theo. Alicia wants to stay just as she is now. She wants to live."

Theo halts. "I see something."

Dale squints, hand over his eyes even though there isn't really sun here, just a perfectly even dull light. A figure running toward them from the distance, getting ever closer. As it approaches, he can see that it's Sara.

She arrives doubled over, hands on her thighs. "Hey."

Theo grabs her by the arm, spins her around. "Did you see Ray?"

She holds up a finger, gasps for breath. "No. But I did see something else."

"Do we have to fucking *beg*?" Theo says, the veins in his neck popping out.

"It's New People. Like a lot of them. We're in some kind of factory."

Dale looks around. "Doesn't look like any kind of factory to me."

Sara tugs at his arm. "This way, jerkass."

As the three of them walk, the scene starts to coalesce into fullness. Long rows of tanks fan out to each side of them, and a low but persistent hum can be both heard and felt. This environment is larger than any scenario he's been in before. It's easily larger than the Boston one. He reaches over and taps on one of the tanks.

A pair of silver eyes stares back at him.

"Jesus!" Dale yells, jumping back. "Are they in all these things?"

"I think it's safe to assume that, yes," Theo says flatly.

Dale cups his hands around his mouth. "Alicia! If you can hear us, do something!"

Sara walks over to a control panel set into the wall and slams her palm down on a group of colorful buttons. Loud sirens and flashing lights surround them.

"What did you do *that* for?"

Sara shrugs. "Better than not doing anything. Hey, where's the black guy?"

"His name is Theo, and he's—" Dale spins around. "Not here." *Shit.*

Sara starts to move down the rows of tanks, and Dale follows. He thinks he hears footsteps, but he doesn't know if it's Theo, Ray, or the beginning of whatever scenario this is. *Please be Theo or Ray,* he thinks.

Static electricity cracks through the air, and when Dale runs his hand over his head, he feels his hair standing on end. Sara's long brown locks have also gone vertical. "I don't like this," she says. "Let's find the tripwire."

"Not when two of us are missing. Theo can't be far." Dale spots a cubicle at the end of the current row of tanks and speeds toward it.

Theo and Ray are thankfully inside, poring over a large binder set on the desk. "Check this out," Ray says. He holds up the binder to show a complete anatomical map of a New Person.

Dale draws a finger down the picture, stopping in the middle where instead of a stomach there's merely a space labeled "power source." *I didn't know they looked like this on the inside,* he thinks. *Well, does it matter?*

"This is a Solfind lab," Theo says, flicking a Post-it emblazoned with the company logo, a setting sun.

"I guess it's where Alicia came from. Where they all came from." There are hundreds of tanks in the lab, but tens of thousands of New People exist already, and more are born every day. A never-ending river of replacements.

Sara's sneakers squeak as she rounds the row of tanks. "I found something weird."

Dale sticks the binder under his armpit and follows her. At the emergency exit door lurks an indistinct shape. He doesn't recognize it as anything at first, but then . . .

"It's that girl we saw in Boston," Ray says.

"Rachel?" Dale reaches out to touch her and connects this time. Streaky bits of his friend come off on his avatar's hand, which he quickly jerks away. "I hope that didn't hurt her."

Theo steps past her toward a metal door, triggering the emergency exit, which leads to another round of sirens. "I'm getting out. You can come if you want."

Sara follows him immediately and then Ray, though Dale guesses that it's less curiosity and more of a desire not to be separated from his husband again. Finally, so does Dale.

The glare of the outer world burns their eyes, and the four of them all fall down in a heap. The smell of fresh-cut grass blossoms in Dale's nostrils, and he reaches a hand into the soft dirt around him, letting it run through his fingers. Alicia's voice calls out, almost too faintly to perceive.

"They're in here."

16

JESS'S SHOULDER SMACKS THE WINDOW OF THE AUTOMATED CAB AS IT FLIES over yet another pothole. Roads outside of Development Zones rarely get repaired. Louisa's been crying the whole time, and Jess is glad there isn't a human driver.

"Hey, it's not much longer."

"I don't *want* to go to Pittsburgh. I want to stay here. I want my records."

Jess reaches down and grabs her sister's face. "There's nothing *for* us here, Lou. People can still get jobs in Islands. They can't all be gone." *Otherwise*, she thinks, *why do this? Why create a technological paradise and shut the doors to people? What's the endgame?*

Louisa shuts her eyes. "Everything I *need* is in those records."

"You don't know what you're saying."

"Even the Network knows it. That boy you hang out with believes it too." Louisa opens her eyes and looks at Jess with a curious expression. "You've never even tried to visit the other world, have you?"

"I did once. It doesn't work. It's just drugs doing that, Lou, not the music."

"You're wrong." Her sister turns away, watching the darkened landscape slowly roll past. "You need both of them. They work together."

"It's *drugs*, Lou. I don't care how good this 'better world' is. It's not worth killing your brain over."

Louisa presses her face against the glass of her window. Jess wonders how long it's been since her sister has traveled in a car. Jess reaches over and pats her on the back.

I wish I saw what you and Dale see, she admits to herself, *but I don't. I only see the real world. It's all I have.* That's why she has to get into a Development Zone. Jess *can't* escape like they can.

Up ahead, a spray of lights covers the unimproved highway. It's a trail of vehicles of all different shapes and sizes, moseying along. At the head of the line, a van painted with whorls of primary colors inches along. Jess instantly recognizes it. "Stop the car," Jess says.

"I have been set on a preordained route," comes the flat voice of the automated driver.

"*Override.*" The car rolls to a stop. Jess can almost swear it feels reluctant.

She opens the door, motioning to Louisa to stay inside. The caravan has stopped too, and a few heads have popped out of windows.

"William!" she yells.

A middle-aged woman steps out of the lead car. "Is there a problem?"

Jess holds up her phone to illuminate the woman's face. "I need to talk to William." Jess looks past the woman's shoulder. "Is he here?"

The woman goes to a car farther down the line, argues for a bit with the driver and walks back. "He says he doesn't know you."

Jess supposes this woman's answers will work just as well. "Why do you listen to Johnny Eternal's music? Why is it playing all the time? It's even playing now." She points to one of the cars where a tinny melody drifts from an open window.

"*I've come so far,*" sings Johnny Eternal, strumming a two-chord progression, "*the final step . . .*" Then the music is engulfed by the sound of a stalled engine.

"We have a very busy schedule, miss. We need to get to Youngstown by tomorrow."

"You travel to the better world with it, don't you?"

Despite the dark, Jess can see the woman's face soften. "You could say that."

Why can't I see it? Jess thinks. *Am I just stupid? Do you have to be this pure to ride the enlightenment express?* "Can people travel with you if they *don't* hear it? If they don't go to the other world?"

"All are welcome," the woman says, though the cross expression on her face doesn't look very welcoming. "Be careful. You're in the middle of the road."

"No traffic anyway," Jess mutters. She goes back to the automated cabbie. "Change course." She gives it the address to Dale's apartment complex.

"What were you doing?" Louisa says accusingly.

"I'm getting us both out," she says. "But first I need to say goodbye."

—\/\/\—

When the cab gets to Dale's apartment building, there's already a cop car waiting outside, its lights flashing. She pays the driver and runs inside, Louisa following.

Dale's friend Rachel is waiting on the front steps, a twentysomething guy Jess doesn't recognize standing next to her. Rachel jumps up, hands already fluttering.

"Jess? You made it? Dale told me before that you weren't coming. He seemed pretty bummed about it."

"The cops," Jess says, pointing back at the car. "Why are there *cops* here? Oh never mind, I'll just go up myself."

"It's Terry," the teenager says. "He came over here to beat Dale up for some reason, and the robot broke his arm."

"Alicia?" But neither one of them register the name.

Rachel gets in front of Jess again. "They're taking Terry to the clinic and then to jail, I think. He was acting pretty crazy."

Jess swings open the door to Dale's apartment. The New Woman sits on his threadbare carpet, its knees drawn up to its chest, its hands encircling them. One of the gaming wires is still held between its teeth.

Jess doesn't say anything to the New Woman, just steps over to where Dale and his new friends twitch on their mats, the wires in their mouths and the helmets on their heads. The stereo plays—what else?—Johnny Eternal.

Louisa flops down on the couch, humming the dissonant song.

"Dale?" Jess whispers, her head only a few inches from his face.

"You shouldn't wake him up," Louisa says.

Jess casts a backward glance at her sister. "I know that." She walks into Dale's kitchen and rummages around for a pen and paper. "I'll just have to leave a note."

The record flips over. One of the two older men makes a loud keening noise. Finally, the letter is done.

"Come on, Lou."

"Are we going home?"

"We're going to a better home." Jess will probably never really know the secrets of the Network or of Johnny Eternal. But she's willing to learn.

"What about Mom?"

"She'll get over it."

Alicia's standing now, her face turned toward Jess and Louisa.

"You can tell Kathy I'm not coming back. I won't be in this state by this time tomorrow."

"Neither will I," the New Woman says. "Solfind is coming to pick me up."

A nameless sensation rises in Jess's body. "Did Terry call them?"

"I did. I'm done with the nightmares. And with endangering people. I'm sure they traced my location anyway after I gave him that money."

"Money?"

Alicia gets to her feet and pops the wire out of her mouth. "A present. Something he needs, and I don't."

Well, that's sketchy as hell, Jess thinks. She points at Alicia's forehead. "So they're in there now? What does it feel like?"

"Like bugs," Alicia says with a near-shudder. "Bugs crawling underneath my skin."

There's an awkward pause, and Louisa pipes up. "Hi."

Alicia drops down to Louisa's level. "Hello there. Your sister says you're going on a trip."

Louisa looks up at Jess, and Jess squeezes her little sister's shoulder. "I'm sorry everything worked out this way," Jess says to Alicia. "I'm sorry you didn't get what you wanted by coming out here."

"I had an adventure," the woman-thing says. Its diction is nearly human now, its motions fluid and natural. "That's more than most of us get to have."

Both kinds of us, Jess thinks, *the real and the synthetic.* She picks up the suitcases and takes Dale's keys from the hook by the door; Alicia's eyebrows rise. "If I ever get back to Pittsburgh, I'll look you up," she lies.

"Don't bother. It won't be me in this body. I've had too many adventures."

Jess hurries Louisa down the steps toward Dale's truck parked at the curb. "What does she mean?" Louisa whispers.

"Never you mind," Jess says. "We've got a caravan to catch."

17

DALE UNTANGLES HIS LEGS FROM WHERE THEY'RE PINNED UNDERNEATH Sara's arms. He stands and squints at the landscape around him. They're in a field, the sun burning hotly but not too brightly overhead. The air is dry and smells sweet.

"Where are we?" Sara asks.

Dale spins around. "Well, still inside Alicia *obviously*."

"It should have worn off by now," Ray says. He slaps at his own face a couple of times. "Why hasn't it worn off?!"

"Alicia, if you're listening, we need to go now." Dale directs his statement to the sky, though there's no way of knowing if she's there or in the ground or not around at all.

"I'm officially terrified," Sara says, wrapping her arms around herself.

"I found water!" Dale turns his head to find Theo about fifty yards away near a small stream.

The others reach the stream. It glistens with an otherworldly light and seems to stretch on forever, past flowers and grasses, before disappearing behind a small hillock almost beyond the limit of Dale's vision.

Sara groans. Theo and Ray hold hands. Dale points. "We might as well follow it."

—⋀⋀⋀—

When they reach the rise of land, it's almost dark. Dale doesn't know why he expected there wouldn't be any night here, but he was clearly mistaken.

"We should stop," Sara says.

"Are you tired? I'm not tired," Ray says.

"We can't just keep walking. We're getting farther and farther away from where we came from." Sara's voice is edgy, almost panicked.

Dale wonders what happened to Rachel's ghost, whether it had just vanished or if she's somehow guiding them, watching over them. Or if Alicia is as well.

Theo lays down on the grass. "I'm not tired, but I wouldn't mind a little rest."

Sara walks over to the stream and miserably slumps down beside it. "We're trapped. They killed the rescue bot—"

"Her name is Alicia," Dale says.

"Whatever. We're stuck here. Just like your friend was."

Dale picks a blade of grass and rubs it between his fingers. "She was okay though. We all saw her. She was okay and wanted to be here with us."

Sara quietly begins to weep. "I can't stay here forever, Dale. No offense, but you're not the three people I want to spend the rest of my life with."

"The feeling is mutual," says Ray.

"We'll start up again in the morning," Dale says. "Maybe we'll find something then."

Nobody makes a sound for the rest of the night, but nobody sleeps either.

During the next day, the sun high in the sky and a slight wind singing over the grass, they spot a small village. One-story houses built close to the ground dot the landscape, and from a distance, they can see others moving like ants.

Sara breaks off at a run.

"Wait!" Dale yells. "Wait for us!" He starts to chase her, to reach the village first to make sure it's safe, to protect all of them. But she's already way out of his reach.

"Hold up," Theo says. He pulls Dale backward. "We have time."

"But . . ." Dale gestures toward the village but finally decides to travel slowly with Theo and Ray.

When they get there, they find Sara in the middle of a group of villagers, short of breath. She holds a finger up to Dale, telling him to wait.

Dale corners a villager. The woman's image is glitchy and unclear, not unlike the way Rachel had appeared all those times before. He wonders if he looks the same to them.

"What is this place?"

She says something that he can't hear and returns to Sara's side. Dale spins back around to Theo and Ray.

"Haven't you figured it out?" Ray says. "They're all players in the game. Just like us."

Dale looks back and considers. Some of the players seem to communicate with one another quite well through speech like the four of them. But mostly, they use signs to talk to one another, bridging the gap.

The ones who are talking came through together, Dale thinks. *Just like me, Sara, Theo, and Ray. This has happened to a lot of people.* He wonders if they all came through Alicia. Maybe she'd lied about never having players in her head before.

Or maybe it's another New Person. There's no way to tell.

Theo and Ray go down to sit among the other players, the ghost people, but Dale hangs back. He's not sure why.

—⎓⎓—

The fuzzy villagers spend their days in quiet contemplation, hands either folded or signing to the other groups. By his second day in the village, Dale notices the same serene look on Sara's face.

They don't need to eat. They don't need to sleep. It's a form of so-called existence, mind-numbing in the extreme, and Dale feels his contempt grow like a cancerous tumor under his avatar's skin.

"Do you think Sara's really happy here?" Dale says to Ray. The older man is wading in the stream, the water up to his shins.

Ray furrows his brow. "You mean you aren't?"

"It's not real. It's like a game except there's no objective." *And no end,* he thinks.

"It's peaceful here." Ray wades out to a deeper part and dunks his head. His longish blond locks emerge drenched, and Ray himself looks utterly tranquil. Just like Sara.

Dale casts a glance toward the ramshackle houses, which aren't necessary. The villagers don't even use them most of the time, and they seem mostly there to mark this spot out as a gathering place. "This place sucks."

"Don't you get it, man?" Ray replies. "This is what we've been looking for. It's what Johnny talks about in the records. It's where we go when we're on Trancium and not hooked up to the game. This *is* the better world."

"It can't be. It's not finished."

A flicker of doubt crosses Ray's face. "Close enough."

—\W—

Everyone but Dale chooses to stay.

"But *why*?" Dale says, aware he's whining. "Sara, I thought you wanted to find the way out. You guys too."

"This is close enough," says Sara. She signs a little to one of the other villagers. "You should stay here too. You're not going to find anything better out there." She sweeps a hand over the endless vista.

"Or if you do, it'll be just like this," Theo says. "They say we're in a holding pattern."

Heat rises to Dale's face. "Holding for *what*? We have to be holding for something."

The three shrug almost in unison. Even though the glitches and voice difficulties aren't there with these three, Dale feels as distant from them now as he does the other villagers.

"Fine. Do what you want. I'm going to explore."

"You can find us again if you need to," says Sara. "Just follow the stream."

Dale grunts and walks away, purposely avoiding the little stream that had led them to the village.

—\W—

A steady progression of dark and light periods marches across the cloudless sky, and at a certain point, Dale's mind breaks. Nearly catatonic, he collapses in a pile in yet another lush glen in this never-changing digital world.

He claws at the dirt. It yields to his touch, and before long, Dale's dug himself a grave. He lies down, waiting for a death that will never come.

Where am I now in reality? Are we dead and discarded, sent to a mass grave? Are we lying in some defunded hospital ward, feeding tubes down our throats?

He senses that it isn't any of those things, and that feels even worse somehow.

For being in her head this long, Dale hasn't thought much about Alicia, but he does so now. Had she survived? Had they *actually* taken down Solfind? Probably not. He nobly tells himself that he'd do all of this again but then decides that, no, he wouldn't.

Day passes to night and night to day. The boundaries between Dale and this strange world begin to blur, and eventually consciousness recedes. The intervals between day and night get shorter with every pass until the sky above him is a flat gray.

And then there is a sound. It's Johnny Eternal's signature ballad, "Fate Found Me," ringing out over the hills and grasses. Dale comes to his senses and hoists himself over the grave onto the flat land, the music swelling around him like an orchestra.

Fate found me by the river
Down my back I felt a shiver
As she reached into my soul and took a piece . . .

He breathes in deeply. He looks up at the sun, feeling it warm his face, suddenly static after untold eons of gray. The song ends and another starts, and Dale finds himself singing along.

"She pinned me on the ground and said I would be bound for the promised land that not all men can see . . ."

Dale chases the music, light on his feet, the whole environment around him changing, becoming more real every minute. Rain begins to fall, and it's the sweetest sensation he can imagine.

He spots a stream. He doesn't know if it's *his* stream, the one that led the four of them to the village back when there were four of them. But it doesn't matter. It will lead him to something. All roads lead everywhere in this impossible place.

Dale Carter skips along—actually skips—on his way to Paradise.

18

WHEN DALE'S TRUCK LIMPS INTO YOUNGSTOWN, THE CARAVAN IS ALREADY packing up. They never stay in one place too long.

It's how they survive, Jess thinks, gazing over the scene through the broken driver's side window. She's had stale air in her mouth these last hundred miles.

Louisa rubs the sleep out of her eyes and pouts. "You got lost a lot."

"You try driving on these roads," Jess says. She starts to pocket the keys but decides to leave them in the door. The truck's about dead anyway. She takes Louisa's hand, and for once, her sister doesn't wince at the touch.

She walks up to the lead vehicle, unsure of how to proceed. William is nowhere in sight, but this isn't about him. This is about her and Louisa, about their *future.*

What do I say? she thinks. *Oh, hi there. Can I join you? With no skills and no real love for Johnny Eternal?* Jess starts to wonder if this was just a terrible idea but then steals a glimpse at Louisa. She's practically quivering with excitement, her head whipping around to take in all the details.

One of the women who'd been juggling fire that night spots her. "You there!" She walks over—around her bare midriff is a tattoo of a snake chasing a fish. "If you came to see the show, you've already missed it."

"'Pisces and Python'," Louisa says, pointing at the woman's navel. "From *Down on Thirty.* His first album."

"My sister and I came all the way from Wheeling," Jess says, barreling ahead before she can change her mind, "to see if we can join you. William invited us."

"He joined up with another group going down South," the woman says. Jess feels her face fall. "But sure, you can come with. Got a vehicle?"

Jess shakes her head. "None that would survive the trip."

"Wait here. I'll figure out who has room."

Louisa bubbles up with so much excitement that Jess can feel it radiating off her. Jess steps away slightly and takes out her phone to make one final, important call. *They might confiscate it,* she thinks. She hadn't noticed any of the Network members using phones.

She redials Dale, who according to the log has called her thirty-one times over the past day and a half of traveling.

"You stole my truck!"

"*Hello,* Dale."

"What the . . . where *are* you, Jess?"

She watches Louisa play some kind of hand-slapping game with a few of the Network kids, no longer sucked down inside the great well of herself. "Sorry about the truck. It was unavoidable. I just wanted to see if you made it out of the game."

"Of *course,* I made it out. What are you talking about?"

"Have you heard from Alicia?"

She can almost hear his shrug. "Nope. Guess she went back to Pittsburgh after all."

"I can't talk long. And I won't be seeing you for a while. Maybe a *long* while."

"Are you in trouble?"

The farthest thing from it, she thinks. "Do you remember what you saw in there? Was it enough to take down Solfind?"

"It's weird," says Dale with a slight hitch in his voice. "I've played dozens of games, but this is the first one that feels hazy. Like a memory of a memory. I can't recall any part of it."

"That's too bad."

"And I feel . . . weird, you know? Like part of my mind is elsewhere. Maybe I should lay off the Trancium for a while. It's almost gone anyway."

"Did you get paid at least?" She considers asking him about Alicia's money comment but decides not to. It's hardly important now.

"Not a goddamn thing."

Jess spots two men from the Network, walking toward her. "That sucks. Anyway, gotta go. I'll be back someday."

"Wait, Jess—" but she's already hung up.

"I'm ready," she says, facing the members. "I'm ready to go now."

They smile serenely like a pair of monks from some obscure order. Which seems pretty close to being the truth. "We have space for you and your sister in vehicle six. Right over there."

Jess calls to her sister, takes her by the hand, and leads her home.

૪

Erica L. Satifka's short fiction has appeared in *Clarkesworld*, *Interzone*, and the anthology *Weird World War III*, among other places. Her debut novel *Stay Crazy* won the 2017 British Fantasy Award for Best Newcomer. Originally from western Pennsylvania, she now lives in Portland, Oregon, with her husband/editor Rob and several adorable talking cats.

BROKEN EYE BOOKS

Sign up for our newsletter at
www.brokeneyebooks.com

Welcome to Broken Eye Books! Our goal is to bring you the weird and funky that you just can't get anywhere else. We want to create books that blend genres and break expectations. We want stories with fascinating characters and forward-thinking ideas. We want to keep exploring and celebrating the joy of storytelling.

If you want to help us and all the authors and artists that are part of our projects, please leave a review for this book! Every single review will help this title get noticed by someone who might not have seen it otherwise.

And stay tuned because we've got more coming . . .

OUR BOOKS

The Hole Behind Midnight, by Clinton J. Boomer
Crooked, by Richard Pett
Scourge of the Realm, by Erik Scott de Bie
Izanami's Choice, by Adam Heine
Never Now Always, by Desirina Boskovich
Pretty Marys All in a Row, by Gwendolyn Kiste
Queen of No Tomorrows, by Matt Maxwell
The Great Faerie Strike, by Spencer Ellsworth
Catfish Lullaby, by A.C. Wise
Busted Synapses, by Erica L. Satifka

COLLECTIONS

Royden Poole's Field Guide to the 25th Hour, by Clinton J. Boomer
Team Murderhobo: Assemble, by Clinton J. Boomer

ANTHOLOGIES
(edited by Scott Gable & C. Dombrowski)
By Faerie Light: Tales of the Fair Folk
Ghost in the Cogs: Steam-Powered Ghost Stories
Tomorrow's Cthulhu: Stories at the Dawn of Posthumanity
Ride the Star Wind: Cthulhu, Space Opera, and the Cosmic Weird
Welcome to Miskatonic University: Fantastically Weird Tales of Campus Life
It Came from Miskatonic University: Weirdly Fantastical Tales of Campus Life
Nowhereville: Weird Is Other People
Whether Change: The Revolution Will Be Weird

Stay weird.
Read books.
Repeat.

brokeneyebooks.com
twitter.com/brokeneyebooks
facebook.com/brokeneyebooks
instagram.com/brokeneyebooks
patreon.com/brokeneyebooks

BROKEN
EYE
BOOKS

CPSIA information can be obtained
at www.ICGtesting.com
Printed in the USA
LVHW051514201020
669305LV00004B/1035

9 781940 372587